"Something I Can Do For You?"

Her voice was deep and husky, and played along Chance's nerve endings in a provocative manner. "I'm Chance Saxon."

"Saxon?" Cleo's smile was surprised, but she extended her right hand. "I'm Cleo North. Very glad to meet you, Mr. Saxon."

Chance took her hand, and felt the firmness and sureness of the woman's grip. "Do you live here?"

Cleo's smile broadened. "I'm your foreman, Mr. Saxon."

"My foreman?" A lady foreman? A forewoman?

Chance was taken aback. His inexperience wouldn't be too detrimental with good help on the place, and he knew he would learn quickly. But he couldn't possibly have imagined working with a woman, especially one whose sexy voice and long legs were already giving him ideas of a personal nature.

The Saxon Brothers: Chance, Rush and Cash— three sinfully sexy brothers who would turn any woman's head!

D0482821

Dear Reader,

Welcome to March and to Silhouette Desire! Our *Man of the Month, Wrangler's Lady,* is from an author many of you have told me is one of your favorites: Jackie Merritt. But this story isn't *just* a *Man of the Month,* it's also the first book in Jackie's exciting new series, THE SAXON BROTHERS.

Next: HAWK'S WAY *is back!* Joan Johnston continues her popular series with *The Cowboy Takes a Wife,* where we learn all about Faron Whitelaw's— from *The Cowboy and the Princess*—half brother, Carter Prescott.

The tie-ins and sequels just keep on coming, with Raye Morgan's *The Daddy Due Date*—a tie-in to last month's *Yesterday's Outlaw*—and BJ James's *The Hand of an Angel,* which continues her terrific books about the McLachlan brothers.

If you're looking for something completely different, you *must* pick up *Carolina on My Mind* by Anne Marie Winston. Here, our hero and heroine are abducted by aliens . . . and that's just for starters! And if you're looking for *humor,* don't miss *Midnight Ice* by Cathie Linz.

Miniseries and tie-ins, bold men and adventurous heroines, the supernatural and humor . . . there's something for *everyone* here at Silhouette Desire. So enjoy.

All the best,

Lucia Macro
Senior Editor

Please address questions and book requests to:
Reader Service
U.S.: P.O. Box 1325, Buffalo, NY 14269
Canadian: P.O. Box 1050, Niagara Falls, Ont. L2E 7G7

JACKIE MERRITT
WRANGLER'S LADY

SILHOUETTE *Desire*®
Published by Silhouette Books
America's Publisher of Contemporary Romance

SILHOUETTE BOOKS

ISBN 0-373-05841-1

WRANGLER'S LADY

Printed in U.S.A.

Books by Jackie Merritt

Silhouette Desire

Big Sky Country #466
Heartbreak Hotel #551
Babe in the Woods #566
Maggie's Man #587
Ramblin' Man #605
Maverick Heart #622
Sweet on Jessie #642
Mustang Valley #664
The Lady and the Lumberjack #683
Boss Lady #705
Shipwrecked! #721
Black Creek Ranch #740
A Man Like Michael #757
Tennessee Waltz #774
Montana Sky #790
Imitation Love #813
†*Wrangler's Lady* #841

†Saxon Brothers series

JACKIE MERRITT

and her husband live just outside of Las Vegas,
Nevada. An accountant for many years, Jackie has
happily traded numbers for words. Next to family,
books are her greatest joy. She started writing in 1987,
and her efforts paid off in 1988 with the publication of
her first novel. When she's not writing or enjoying a
good book, Jackie dabbles in watercolor painting and
has been known to tickle the ivories in her spare time.

Prologue

"**D**id you know anything at all about it before today?" Cash Saxon asked his older brother.

Chance shook his head. "Not a hint." He looked at his two brothers, Cash and Rush, and saw the same stunned emotions on their faces that he was feeling inside. They were standing on the sidewalk amidst a swirl of pedestrians, just outside of the large sedate building which housed the law firm of Teale, Fitch and McGruder. "Come on. I'll buy you both a drink. I think we could use one."

The cocktail lounge was dimly lighted and cool. There was music, something with an easy beat, coming from concealed speakers. The brothers bypassed vacant tables for one in a corner, distancing themselves from the lounge's other patrons. A waitress appeared. Drinks were ordered. The three Saxon men, tight-lipped and tense, sat without speaking until their drinks were delivered.

Chance raised his Scotch and spoke wryly. "Stay cool, you two. It only feels like the end of the world." He took a big swallow.

Two weeks ago they had been summoned home to Manhattan. *Come at once. Your grandfather gravely ill.* Chance had been in Australia, Cash in California and Rush in France. They had all arrived in time to speak a few words to their grandfather before he died, although they would never know if he had heard and understood.

Today they had met with Robert Teale, the family attorney, for the reading of the will. Hearing they were close to penniless when money had barely been a consideration all of their lives, let alone a problem, was a shock they were still feeling.

"There's very little left of the Saxon fortune," Cash said grimly. "It's almost impossible to believe."

"We did our best to spend it," Rush drawled dryly.

Chance pulled a small sheaf of papers from his coat pocket. "This is what's left, three financially strapped businesses in..." He glanced at the top sheet. "Oregon, Montana and Nevada."

They were impeccably dressed, handsome dark-haired men, tall and lean. At thirty-four Chance was the oldest; Cash was thirty-two, Rush was thirty. The family resemblance was strong as all three had inherited their mother's beauty, altered to masculinity by their father's rugged frame and features.

But they knew their parents more from photos than memory; Deirdre and Rupert Saxon had died in a plane crash when their sons were one, three and five years of age. The boys had been raised by their grandfather, adored and indulged by the old gentleman. Now they were not only faced with soul-deep grief over losing their beloved granddad, but also the only life-style they knew was no longer available.

Chance looked at his brothers over the rim of his glass. He was not their leader. Cash and Rush were as strong-willed as himself. Growing up, they had fought like tigers with each other, and then united and fought against anything that threatened any one of them.

But someone had to do something. All three of them were stunned and aimless, and they couldn't afford to be. Not for long, at any rate. Chance took it upon himself, being the eldest, to instigate a discussion with some purpose.

"I'd like to make a suggestion." Cash and Rush had been staring into their drinks, and they raised their eyes hopefully. Chance laid the sheaf of papers on the table and then tapped them. "We have these," he said, meaning the businesses listed. "They might not be much, but they're a place to start."

"There's barely enough cash to make the trip west," Rush said.

"My point exactly," Chance replied. "If we stay here and do nothing, that'll be gone, too."

"I still can't believe everything's gone." Cash sighed. "The house, the yacht, the polo ponies."

Chance winced. Losing the polo ponies was a particularly tough cross to bear for him. He'd grown up loving horses and had just naturally gravitated to polo.

Pain made him caustic. "We can't sit around crying in our beer—Scotch," he amended wryly and began to shuffle through the papers. "There's a house construction company in Las Vegas, Nevada, a logging operation in the Cascade Mountains of Oregon, and a cattle ranch near Kidd River, Montana. I think we should each take one and..."

"Take one!" Cash snorted. "And do what with it? What do any of us know about running a business?"

"We're not stupid, Cash," Chance said coolly. "I'm not going to sit on my hands and hope the attorneys are wrong, are you?"

No one said anything. Looks were exchanged. The reality of their situation grew in each man. Cash finally nodded, albeit grimly. "Teale doesn't make mistakes and we may as well face it. All right, I'm game. Who goes where?"

Another silence ensued. They were thinking, weighing the options.

Rush spoke, rather tentatively. "The desert appeals to me, if that means anything."

"It makes as much sense as anything else going on right now," Chance replied. "Fine, you go to Nevada. Cash? Oregon or Montana?"

"You're the equestrian. The Montana cattle ranch would be best for you. I'll take Oregon."

"You're sure?"

"I like the West Coast. I'll take Oregon," Cash confirmed.

"Then it's settled." Chance raised his hand to draw the waitress's attention. "Another round over here, please." He grinned dryly at his brothers. "This time we'll toast the future and wish each other luck. I have a feeling we're all going to need it."

One

The Saxon brothers made one more group decision before going their separate ways: They would show up at their chosen destinations without announcement or fanfare.

Chance flew into Helena, Montana, rented a car and followed a map on a northwesterly course. He'd never even heard of Kidd River before, but then his grandfather had shared few details of the Saxons' source of wealth. Chance did a lot of thinking about that during the flight west, wondering why the old man had kept so much to himself. He'd seen to his grandsons' education, expensive schools, of course, and then given them free rein to roam the globe. The three of them—Chance, Cash and Rush—were professional travelers, if little else.

In truth, Chance was more worried about his brothers than he was about himself. At least he understood horses, which there were bound to be on a cattle ranch. But what did Cash know about logging, or Rush about construction?

Pulling over at a crossroad to study the map, Chance took time to look at the area. It was July and hot. To the west were the Rockies, treed and towering, but on the flats the dun-colored grass went on for miles in every direction. There weren't any fences that he could see, not in this particular location. He'd driven past fences, of course, and through small towns, past isolated clumps of buildings, ranches, obviously, and wandering cattle, seemingly untended, with an occasional roadside sign warning travelers of open-grazing and to watch for animals.

For some reason he hadn't expected Montana to resemble the Australian outback, and it didn't if one made precise comparisons. But there were similarities: very few people, for one, and a feeling of aloneness that was strangely strengthening. Chance had spent several months exploring Australia and had met some remarkable people. He wondered if he would find the same pronounced sense of self in Montanans that he had admired as characteristic of so many Australians.

After studying the map again, he made a left turn and found himself driving on a gravel road. There was another turn and then another, and finally he approached the Saxons' Kidd River Ranch, squatting, so it seemed, on prairie land that rolled into mountains not more than five or six miles from its hind side. Its nearest neighbor had to be a good ten miles away, and the small town of Kidd River, which Chance had slowed down for, briefly, was at least thirty miles back.

He stopped the car again to survey his new home from a distance. The house was tall and narrow and constructed of rock, a very old house by the look of it. There was an immense wooden barn and several other outbuildings. He counted five parked vehicles next to the house, and there were cattle, although there was so much land the animals were strung out, far afield of each other. Chance spotted some horses and squinted his eyes to see them better. He shook his head because they seemed ordinary, nothing at all like the sleek ponies he was accustomed to riding.

He drove on slowly, his forehead soberly creased. The placid scenery of mountains, plains and enormous blue sky were moving. This was his future, this vast silent country, but was he capable of meeting its challenge? He and his brothers had agreed to help each other with their diverse ventures wherever possible, but Cash and Rush would have their hands full in Nevada and Oregon, and there was little question in Chance's mind that he was now on his own.

Reaching the complex, he parked near the other vehicles and got out. The stone house was by far the most interesting structure, and Chance was drawn to it. Standing at a wall, he placed a hand on the pale rocks and realized he was looking at quarried stone.

"It was built in the thirties," a voice behind him stated. Chance turned to see a woman. "There used to be a quarry about five miles downriver," she said. "There are about a dozen buildings still standing in the area constructed of the same stone."

Chance took in the woman's long legs in snug, faded denim, the soft-leather scuffed boots on her feet and the old hat that concealed most of her hair—a golden color, he saw from the visible sections above her ears. Her skin was smooth and the color of light honey. She wore a plaid cotton shirt with the sleeves rolled up, and the green of her eyes had the depth and coolness of a mountain lake.

Her eyes also contained a question, which she promptly shared. "Something I can do for you?"

Her voice was deep and husky, and played along Chance's nerve endings in a provocative manner. "I'm Chance Saxon."

"Saxon?" Cleo's smile was surprised, but she extended her right hand. "I'm Cleo North. Very glad to meet you, Mr. Saxon."

Chance took her hand, and felt the firmness and sureness of the woman's grip. "Do you live here?"

Cleo's smile broadened. "I'm your foreman, Mr. Saxon."

"My foreman?" A lady foreman? A fore*woman*?

"You didn't know?"

"No." Chance was taken aback. His inexperience wouldn't be too detrimental with good help on the place, and he knew he would learn quickly. But he couldn't possibly have imagined working with a woman, especially one whose sexy voice and long legs were already giving him ideas of a personal nature.

"I've worked here for five years," Cleo stated. "I've been foreman for three." Her elation over a Saxon finally showing up was still present. The ranch was in trouble, and a member of the wealthy Saxon family actually coming to see it firsthand was an answer to her prayers. She hadn't visualized any of the Saxons having such deep blue eyes, however. Nor almost black, luxurious hair and a long, lean physique. His clothing was casual, jeans, boots and shirt, although he wore them with a notable flair. Chance Saxon was an unusually handsome man, which seemed strangely out of sync to her, a trifle disturbing.

She glanced at the strange car and saw its Montana plates. "You rented a car? I would have been happy to pick you up, Mr. Saxon."

"Thanks, but I've never been in Montana before and wanted to poke along and absorb the sights."

"Understandable." It occurred to Cleo that Saxon's visit might be very short-lived, in which case the rental car would provide him with transportation back to Helena and the airport. "Would you like to bring in your things?" she asked.

"Might as well," Chance concurred. "Who owns all these vehicles?" he asked as they wound through them to reach his car.

"You own two of them, that blue pickup and the black Blazer. The gray van is mine. The other pickups belong to the hired help."

"Two people? Men?"

Cleo's smile contained an amused understanding. "The cook and all-around handyman, Joe Biggins, and our one cowhand, Pete Dolaski."

"Only one cowhand?"

"That's all we can afford, Mr. Saxon. This time of year isn't so crucial, but come fall roundup we'll have to put on extra help."

Chance thought of the briefcase crammed with reports on the ranch provided by Robert Teale. He hadn't yet had the time to study the information, but doing so was a high-priority item, he realized.

Unlocking the trunk, he lifted the door. Cleo's eyes widened, because not only was it crammed full of suitcases, but she could see that the car's back seat was also loaded. What really surprised her were the skis, the golf clubs and the tennis rackets, all in costly leather travel bags. Apparently this *wasn't* a brief visit, not if Saxon's luggage was any measure.

But what on earth did he plan to do with tennis rackets and golf clubs? Ski slopes weren't that far away, although it was hardly the season for skiing, but the nearest golf course was in Helena, and no one she knew played tennis.

Then it struck her: Chance Saxon was on vacation! This was merely a duty call because he was in the area. Cleo's system rebelled and she gritted her teeth. Didn't this ranch mean anything to that family?

Chance began transferring luggage from the trunk to the ground. Cleo picked up two suitcases, and he frowned. "You don't have to carry those. They're heavy."

"Heavy?" Cleo glanced down at the two elegant black leather pieces in her hands. Her expression became droll. "Believe me, they're not nearly as heavy as a bale of hay, Mr. Saxon."

For a moment Chance watched her walking off, then he quickly tucked his briefcase under his left arm and picked up two suitcases. Following Cleo North to the house, he found himself watching her behind. It didn't sway, it didn't look soft, and yet it was the neatest display of female pulchritude he could recall witnessing. Cleo moved with a tight precision that appeared natural and effortless. Her straight back was every bit as appealing as her firm hips and long legs, and the indentation of her waist, marked by an inch-wide leather belt, seemed to Chance like the purest expression of womanhood.

He gave his head a shake. Getting ditzy ideas about his foreman—fore*woman*—when he didn't even know if she was married, had to be the height of absurdity. He liked women and there was usually one on the scene. But his entire future depended on this enterprise, and muddying the already cloudy waters with a romantic entanglement would definitely be a step in the wrong direction.

Cleo went into the house calling, "Joe?"

A small, wizened man wearing an apron appeared. "Yeah?"

"Chance Saxon, Joe Biggins," Cleo said.

Chance put down his load to shake hands. "You one of the Saxons?" Joe questioned over the handshake. Chance grinned, and Cleo saw his embarrassment as oddly endearing, which made her stiffen her spine. The man was her employer, for Pete's sake. "'Bout time one of you showed your face 'round here," Joe added bluntly.

"Guess it is," Chance agreed, and cast Cleo a doubtful glance. She rolled her eyes, hoping to convey that Joe's outspokenness was put up with because good, reliable cooks weren't all that plentiful.

"Come along," she said to Chance. "I'll show you where you can hang your hat while you're here."

Chance took in the house as they walked through it. The ceilings were unusually high, giving the rooms a long, narrow appearance, an impression that was reinforced by long, narrow windows. The floor was hardwood planking, varnished and smooth and protected in traffic areas with lengths of carpet. The living room, he saw, contained a huge fireplace constructed of the same stone used on the outside of the house.

He followed Cleo up the stairs and then down a hall. "There are four bedrooms up here," she told him. "You can have your pick. No one else stays here."

"What about Joe?"

"Joe has his own small trailer parked down by the river, and Pete stays in the bunkhouse."

"I thought you lived here."

Cleo stopped at the last door in the hall. "I think this is the best room because of the view." She set down a suitcase to open the door. "I live on the ranch, Mr. Saxon, but there's a second house." Preceding him into the room, Cleo deposited Saxon's luggage at the foot of the bed. "I don't live alone."

The strangest disappointment rippled through Chance; she was married.

"I have a daughter," Cleo explained. "Rosie is eight years old."

"And your husband works elsewhere?" Chance added his load of luggage to the other two suitcases at the foot of the bed, and laid his briefcase on the faded blue spread.

"I don't have a husband, Mr. Saxon." Cleo maintained an unflinching gaze. "Never did."

Her meaning sunk in, and after a moment Chance nodded, dismissing the topic. "This room looks fine to me." He walked to a window and peered out. "You're right about the view. The mountains are incredible from here."

"Yes, they are." Cleo thought about Saxon's acceptance of her personal status and felt relief. She preferred being upfront with new acquaintances, though there were circumstances concerning Rosie's birth that couldn't be blurted quite so casually.

Still, it was best, she had decided years ago, that no one she met ever got the idea she was ashamed of having a child and no husband. She was protective of her small daughter and loved her to distraction, and she could never be ashamed of the biggest blessing of her life.

Chance turned from the window. "Downstairs you said something about hanging my hat for as long as I'm here. I'm here to stay, Cleo. May I call you Cleo?"

To stay? "Yes, of course," she murmured absently. "You're here permanently?" There was a touch of disbelief in her voice.

"Permanently," Chance confirmed. He glanced around the room at the old-fashioned decor and furnishings. There was no television set, no stereo, no telephone. "Do we have telephones on the place?"

"Downstairs in the study."

"No extensions?" What about electricity? he thought, and was relieved when his gaze settled on a lamp on the bed stand and then the ceiling light.

"No extensions," Cleo said. And then, because she saw his look of concern, she added, "The bathroom's down the hall. There's only one of those, as well, I'm afraid." Privately she was still trying to assimilate him living here permanently. Despite his Western clothing, there was a polish to Chance Saxon that she had seen only one other time, Rosie's father had exuded a similar sophistication.

The comparison gave her sudden goose bumps. She had vowed to never even look at a man with that sort of devastating charm again, and here was Chance Saxon, a permanent fixture in her life.

Still, she wasn't sorry he had come. Someone had to do something about the ranch's sorry economic state, and only its owners had the authority and financial clout to do so.

They had an enormous amount to discuss, although if Saxon had stayed abreast of the constant flow of reports she mailed back East, he already had an understanding of the ranch's sad history.

"I'll bring in the rest of your things," she said, and started for the door.

Chance jumped. "You'll do no such thing," he rebutted rather sharply.

Cleo stopped. "I work here, Mr. Saxon."

"That doesn't make you a pack horse. *I'll* bring in my things," he said adamantly. "And call me Chance."

"If you wish. But, really, there's no reason why I can't carry in . . ."

Chance held up a hand. "I don't know what you're accustomed to doing around here, but it's not going to be carrying my luggage up a long flight of stairs."

Cleo folded her arms. "I can do anything on this ranch a man can do."

There was a prideful, stubborn tilt to her chin, Chance saw, and a completely unexpected burst of desire hit him with the impact of a fist. He wasn't used to walloping doses of lust, not for women he knew and certainly not for one he'd just met. But an image of laying Cleo North on that bed and peeling away those snug jeans was suddenly giving him a fever and an uncomfortably full feeling in his own jeans.

The bright, hot light in Saxon's blue eyes made Cleo uneasy, and she sidled closer to the door. What was so disturbing was that she recognized what it was and the idea wasn't at all repugnant, certainly nowhere near as unnerving as the sudden pressure in her own system.

"I have things to do," she mumbled at the door.

"Don't let me keep you."

"See you later." One step into the hallway and Cleo stopped. "Supper's at six."

Chance crossed the room to the doorway. "Do you and Rosie eat in the main house?"

"Occasionally, but usually Rosie and I eat in our own quarters."

"Will you join me tonight?"

Cleo braved a direct look at his handsome face. "If you want to talk about the ranch, it would be better to meet after supper. I could come to the study this evening."

"And Rosie?"

"It's summer vacation. Rosie doesn't have to be in bed early, and she'll stay home with her dogs. The house we live in is just across the compound, well within sight."

Chance could hardly believe the agitation in the air. No more than twenty minutes had gone by since their meeting, and he and this woman were both nearly frozen with sexual tension. He wondered what would happen if he touched her, and was tempted to find out.

But a pass would forever alter their standing, which was only just barely getting established. He needed her experience and her knowledge. He was as close to being a fish out of water on this isolated ranch as anyone could be. He might never get over the shock of his foreman being a female, let alone one that could make his hair stand on end. But destroying, or at least delaying, his own future for a quick thrill would be the act of an utter fool, and his days of carelessness were over. They had to be.

Drawing a much needed breath, he stepped back. "See you this evening."

Cleo didn't run down the hall but neither did she dawdle. Chance Saxon was a dangerous man. If he ever followed through with what she'd seen in his eyes, she would have to quit her job and leave the Kidd River Ranch. The thought weakened her knees. She loved this place and had made her daughter and herself a good home here. Rosie couldn't even remember living anywhere else.

Downstairs, Cleo cut through the kitchen. Joe was mixing up a batch of biscuits, which he obviously didn't mind leaving for some conversation. "So...wha'd'ya think of Saxon?"

"I'm glad he's here."

"Well, yeah, but wha'd'ya think of 'im?"

"It's too soon to know. I've got to go. See you later, Joe." Leaving Joe grumbling to himself, Cleo took the back steps two at a time and struck out across the compound.

Chance was at the window of his room again, frowning, looking at the buildings outside, worrying. Worry was a brand-new experience for him. Till recently his only worries had revolved around meeting airline schedules, or whether he should spend July on the Saxon yacht cruising the East Coast or in exploring some cool northern province in Canada. He knew more about the rest of the world than he did about some of the states in his own country, he realized uneasily. Certainly having some knowledge of Montana would make this undertaking easier.

His eyes narrowed suddenly. Cleo was hiking across the compound. What was under that old hat? Was her golden hair short, or long and tucked under the hat?

He watched as she approached a small stone building with a white picket fence separating it from the rest of the compound. A child came bounding around the building with two tan dogs on her heels. Cleo bent down and hugged the child, then they went inside holding hands.

That's where she lived, her and Rosie, in that tiny stone house with a patch of lawn, a white picket fence and two scruffy dogs. There'd been joy in the embrace of mother and daughter, and Chance didn't have to hear laughter to know it had been a part of their greeting. Cleo North was not an unhappy woman, he realized. Her statement about never having had a husband had been neither a bid for sympathy nor an apology. She was that rare breed of person who demanded that people take her as she was or not at all.

Chance rubbed his mouth thoughtfully. This was his life now. He didn't have to stay here, any more than Cash would have to stick with the logging operation in Oregon or Rush would have to deal with the construction company in Nevada.

But if all three ventures became successful, they would be well on their way to starting a second Saxon empire. Why couldn't the three of them do it when their grandfather had been only one person and had succeeded so well?

Chance eyed the briefcase he'd tossed on the bed. Those reports were tonight's reading. Right now, though, he needed to haul in the rest of his things and take a hike around the place.

As for Cleo North, she was a valuable employee. He'd best remember that the next time he started getting silly ideas about laying her down and peeling away her jeans.

Two

"**I**'m going to the big house for a meeting with Mr. Saxon," Cleo told her daughter that evening after the supper dishes were washed and put away.

"Okay, Mama. Can I paint while you're gone?"

"*May* I paint, and yes you may. I'll get you a cup of water." Rosie had a set of watercolors, and her pictures invariably consisted of rainbows and horses. "Try not to spill, okay?"

"I'll try," Rosie solemnly agreed.

Cleo thought Rosie was the most beautiful child ever, and truly, the little girl was a darling with her dark curls and bright blue eyes. She had a sweet, loving disposition, too, reminding Cleo of herself as a youngster, before life's realities began demanding strength and pragmatism. Fantasies were for children, little girls with visions of rainbows, not for a grown woman with a child to raise.

After delivering a large cup of water to the kitchen table, Cleo kissed her daughter's smooth cheek. "I won't be long."

"Turn on the radio, Mama."

"Will do." On her way out, Cleo switched on the radio, which was already dialed to her favorite country-western station. There was very poor television reception in the area, and those scattered ranchers in the area who wanted it had satellite dishes. Cleo didn't miss TV and in fact believed Rosie was developing better without it. Even if she had the extra money to spend, which she didn't as she was putting everything away she could for Rosie's education, she wouldn't buy a satellite dish.

After showering, Cleo had donned a cotton skirt and blouse, which she often did at the end of a hot day. Her hair was clean but no more fussed over than usual. After a shampoo, Cleo merely brushed it back from her face and tied it with a ribbon or whatever was on hand. During working hours, she usually pinned it on top of her head so it would fit under her hat. Down, as it was tonight, it reached several inches below her shoulders.

But there wasn't a speck of makeup on her face and never would be for Chance Saxon, or any other man. There was no perfume at her throat, nothing about her that was any different than normal routine.

And yet she felt like a woman going to meet a man as she strode across the compound toward the big house. It was a ludicrous sensation and annoying. Everyone in the area knew she didn't date, ever, and rarely went anywhere without Rosie. It was strictly by choice. She'd been asked many times, though not for years, she realized. Mainly because she hadn't met anyone new.

Until today.

The house was silent when she went in. Joe had gone to his trailer, obviously, and Pete to the bunkhouse. Chance Saxon was completely alone in this big old house.

Cleo paused in the kitchen to collect herself. Chance struck her as a worldly man, though she really knew next to nothing about the Saxon family. Reports on the ranch regularly went East, but nothing beyond an occasional check ever came West. For three months now, there hadn't been any checks.

She sucked in a deep breath, composed her features and continued through the house to the study door, which had been left open. Chance looked up, then rose from behind the desk. "Come in."

"Thank you." Entering, Cleo went to the chair at the front of the desk and sat down.

Chance tried not to stare, but the woman before him was worthy of any man's undivided attention. Her beauty was as natural as the sun and the stars, and he would bet anything she had done nothing more than bathe and brush her fabulous hair. It shone like a beacon in this drab room with its dark wood and time-faded fabrics.

Cleo recognized the papers strewn across the desk. "You're reading ranch reports."

Resuming his seat, Chance nodded. "For the first time."

Cleo blinked. "I don't understand."

"Probably not, but these reports were given to me only a week ago. In preparing for this trip, there was no time to read anything. I'm trying to catch up." Chance leaned back in his chair. "The ranch is in trouble, isn't it?"

"Yes," Cleo admitted without hesitation. "We're almost out of cash, and there hasn't been any money from Mr. Teale for over three months."

"There won't be any, either."

The bottom seemed to fall out of Cleo's stomach. "Perhaps you should explain."

"There isn't any money, Cleo. The Saxon family is broke."

"But..." She stopped, because there really wasn't anything for her to say.

"I came here hoping to pick up the pieces. I'm the first to admit I can't do it alone, though my foreman being a woman came as no small shock. But I need your help. I don't know the first thing about running a cattle ranch, and you obviously know a lot about it."

"I was raised on a ranch by an aunt and uncle who are both gone now. It was a leased place," Cleo said almost warily, as though she were treading on alien ground and unsure of her footing. Chance Saxon, with neither money nor knowledge, wasn't what this operation needed.

"You said you've worked here for five years."

"Yes. I was living in Billings and trying to juggle caring for Rosie with a job managing a fast-food restaurant. I was making a good salary, but Rosie was being raised by baby-sitters. By accident I heard that the Kidd River Ranch needed a cowhand. I drove out here and spoke with the foreman, Bud Crocker. There were seven full-time employees then, and the ranch was doing very well. The house I live in was being used as a storage shed. It took some talking, but I eventually convinced Bud I could do the job as well as any of his men. He gave me the chance to prove myself and then let me clean up the little house and move in."

"I took a walk around the place before dinner and noticed the bunkhouse is large enough to accommodate a good dozen people," Chance said.

"Which we need during fall roundup and spring branding."

"You said the ranch was doing well five years ago. What happened?"

"It was nearly destroyed three years ago, Chance. Bud Crocker left about eighteen months after I came, and the guy who took his place was a thief. The foreman has access to the ranch's money—someone has to pay the bills—and Lyle disappeared one day and so did nearly two hundred thousand dollars."

Chance's mouth dropped open. "You're not serious."

"I'm afraid so. Anyway, nothing was done about it that I ever heard. That damned sneak Lyle got away with it. God only knows where he is now, but I'd bet anything your money's long gone. The men working on the place at the time didn't know which way to turn, so I came in here to the study and started writing letters back East. That's how I made contact with Robert Teale. He instructed me to take over the operation, which I did. The place never recovered. Mr. Teale's been sending money when I needed it, and this year, I'd like to point out, I've needed much less than last. The first year was very difficult, though, a terrible drain on your family's finances. I'm sorry."

"Don't feel guilty. Believe me, the little that was sent here didn't make a drop in a bucket compared to how my brothers and I went through money."

"Oh, you have brothers."

"Two, Cash and Rush." Chance smiled. "My mother had a vivid imagination when it came to naming her sons."

"Will they be coming out here, too?"

"They've got other fish to fry," Chance answered, feeling a pang at what Cash and Rush might be encountering. Certainly they were as ignorant of Saxon economic history as himself. "Three years is a long time. I'm sure you're right about the money Lyle took being gone, even if we managed to catch up with him at this late date."

Chance got up to wander the room. "I'm not going to waste my time chasing after a thief," he said after a moment of contemplation. "I need to get the feel of this place. Study those reports. Really grasp the cattle business." He looked at Cleo. "You sell the stock in the fall?"

"That's the normal routine. This operation is twofold, Chance. We not only buy and raise young steers for beef, but we also keep cows for breeding and raise our own cattle."

Chance frowned. "Explain a little more."

"There are ranchers who only buy young steers in the spring, put some weight on them and sell in the first or second fall. Kidd River Ranch has always done some of that, but we also maintain a herd of cows to produce our own calves."

"Would you say we have salable animals on the place right now?"

"Yes, of course. Anyone can haul their animals to auction anytime they choose. But this year's purchased steers or home-born calves wouldn't turn a profit yet, and selling the cows would decrease your assets. It's a practice I've avoided."

"But it would bring in some cash," Chance pointed out.

Disliking the idea didn't prevent Cleo from seeing its logic. "Yes, it would."

"I take it we've got bulls?"

Cleo shook her head. "Artificial insemination is cheaper and much more scientific."

Chance couldn't help a wry laugh. "But not nearly as much fun for the cows, right?"

"The bulls, either, I'm sure," Cleo drawled dryly. "From a rancher's standpoint, however, AI makes good sense."

"And just who handles that job?"

Cleo leveled an amused gaze on her employer. "Anyone who's working on the place in August. Cows gestate in nine months, similar to humans. Impregnate in August, new calves in May. It's simple arithmetic."

"And damned distasteful work," Chance growled. "Do you actually take part in it?"

Cleo couldn't help laughing. "Of course I take part in it." Her expression became teasing. "Don't worry. *Someone* has to hold the cow's tail out of the way." She sobered. "Having a woman for a foreman bothers you, doesn't it?"

"You'd better believe it, honey."

At the sudden sensual tone of his voice, Cleo stiffened and got to her feet. "I think we should get something out of the way, Mr. Saxon. I love this place and Rosie has thrived out here. This job is very important to me, but I will never compromise my principles to keep it."

Chance became very still. "Did I suggest otherwise?"

"Not in so many words, no. But..."

"You're offended by my admiration? You're a beautiful woman, Cleo. Don't tell me other men haven't said the same thing to you."

"Not for a very long time, which is how I prefer it." In truth, she considered herself average looking and any such flattery as a line. It was an attitude Chance Saxon might as well hear and understand right at the outset.

"Are you saying you don't..." Chance searched for the right word and settled for "...date?"

"That's precisely what I'm saying." At Chance's look of disapproval, Cleo's expression became knowing. She'd encountered the same response in other men. "And *that* offends you. Why?"

"Because people weren't meant to live alone."

"Are *you* married?" Cleo questioned pointedly.

"No."

"Then your observation isn't exactly based on firsthand experience, is it, Mr. Saxon?"

"You were calling me by my first name a few minutes ago."

"Yes, but maybe it's best if we keep this relationship on a strictly impersonal level. That is, if you still want me here."

"I want you," Chance said coolly, and didn't even attempt to clarify his meaning.

Cleo did it for him. "You want me to continue working for you."

She'd made herself abundantly clear, and visualizing himself trying to run this place without her input had Chance sweating. Until he found someone else who understood the business as well as Cleo did, she had him over the proverbial barrel. He didn't like his position, but then he didn't like a lot of what had been happening recently.

He dropped all pretense and got down to business. "You want it strictly impersonal, that's how it'll be. Tell me what you're doing on the place at the present," he said briskly, and sat behind the desk.

Cleo remained standing, feeling strangely empty. Chance's acquiescence was only what she'd demanded, so why the sudden void in her system?

Shaking off the peculiar sensation, she sat down. "This is the slowest time of year, the season when ranchers in these parts make repairs to their equipment and buildings, or put up new ones. We have a hay crop that will need cutting in about another week. It's dryland hay, but we've had plenty of rain and it's a good crop.''

"We feed the animals during the winter?''

"Six inches of snow on the ground and they go hungry if we don't haul hay. Last winter was mild, but if the coming winter isn't, we'll need more hay than we grow, which is additional expense.''

"So what do you have Pete doing?''

"You met him at supper?''

"Yes.''

"Pete's worked here for two years and knows the ropes. Right now most of our cattle are in the foothills. Pete rides out and checks on them every morning. They're not far, about five or six miles away. When he gets back, depending on the time of day, I put him at one chore or another. Today he serviced the swather. Do you know what a swather is?''

"It cuts and strips the hay,'' Chance said brusquely, a little annoyed that she would think him a total ignoramus. He wanted to ask what she was doing during this "slow" season, but didn't have the nerve.

Cleo filled him in all on her own. "For the past few days I've been riding the riverbank, Mr. Saxon. I mentioned rain, and a hard rain, which we had three days ago, swells the river and creates mud pots in certain areas. We've lost young beeves in those pots, so we always make it a point to check the river after a heavy rainfall. I was just getting back this afternoon when I saw your car driving in.''

"Who watches Rosie when you're away from the compound?''

A smile tipped Cleo's lips. "Rosie rides like a seasoned hand. She goes with me when she's not in school and weather permits. Do you object?''

"And when weather doesn't permit?''

"She stays in the house, of course. Mr. Saxon, my daughter never has nor ever will stop me from doing my job. She's very bright and understands I have to make a living.''

"What about playmates? Does she have any friends her age?"

"Friends come to see her occasionally, but they play within the fence around my house. They will never be a problem, I assure you."

Chance frowned. "You're very defensive. I wasn't thinking of children on the place as a problem. Frankly I was concerned about one small girl being cut off from people her own age for an entire summer."

Embarrassment put color in Cleo's cheeks. "I'm sorry. I am defensive, I know, but only about certain things."

"About Rosie, apparently."

Cleo nodded slightly. "I can't deny it. She's my reason for living."

Taking a slow, speculative breath, Chance regarded the striking woman across the desk. Questions were stacking up in his mind. She hadn't married Rosie's father—why not? And why had she cut herself off from male companionship because of one mistake, if she even saw bearing an out-of-wedlock child as a mistake? Maybe she didn't. She was proud of her daughter, obviously, and extremely protective.

But if Cleo North believed her only reason for living was her child, she was either incredibly self-deluding or very strong-willed. She didn't seem like the sort of person to tell herself lies and then live by them, and he'd already experienced her stubborn will, so maybe that topic needed no further conjecture.

In the next heartbeat Chance realized that he liked Cleo North, a lot. Business only was undoubtedly the best course for both of them, but he was intensely attracted to her. If she ever unbent and gave him an opening, he'd probably take it.

His mood having changed drastically, Chance risked a teasing smile. "Are there other lady wranglers in Montana?"

Cleo's inner response to that smile unnerved her. Chance was too good-looking, too sure of himself. Maybe not with the ranch, but she doubted that he'd struck out with very many women, and he seemed to possess hordes of confidence in his own appeal to the opposite sex.

"There are lots of lady wranglers, as you put it," Cleo said evenly. "Although most women working on ranches are working their own places." She managed a reasonably friendly smile. "Are we through for tonight?"

"Anxious to leave?"

"Not at all. If you have more questions, feel free to ask them."

Chance thought for a moment, then shook his head. "Guess that does it for now. Oh, wait, there is something else. My rental car will have to be returned to the airport in Helena."

Cleo stood up. "I'll have Pete and Joe take care of it tomorrow."

Rising, Chance watched her walk to the door. She hesitated a second and turned. "Do you ride?"

He laughed. "Yeah, I ride. Why?"

"I thought you might enjoy a tour of the outer land, maybe take a look at the cattle in the foothills."

"I'd like that, thanks. In the morning?"

"Right after breakfast."

"And what time is breakfast?"

"At six."

Chance nodded. He'd always been a morning person and would be up before six, in any case. "By the way, where will I find the checkbook and current ledgers?"

"In the third drawer of the file cabinet in that closet." Cleo gestured toward a door between two bookcases. "Everything's up-to-date."

"I'm sure it is," Chance drawled dryly, then tempered the somewhat cynical observation with a smile. "You're a capable woman."

"I'm a capable *person*, Mr. Saxon. My gender is neither a plus nor a minus to this job."

"A debatable point, Cleo. See you in the morning."

When she had gone, Chance sank into his chair. He had one hell of a lot of homework and might as well get at it.

What surprised him was his own unexpected eagerness to
know, to study, to learn. His thus far cursory examination
of Cleo's reports was disheartening, true, but already the
place was becoming real to him. If Cash and Rush were
fortunate enough to feel the same thing about their ventures, all three of them just might do all right.

He was going to give it his all, Chance realized. He might
have spent the first thirty-four years of his life in the pursuit of pleasure, but that was over and he no longer rued its
passing. To be honest, the challenge of the Kidd River
Ranch was the most exciting and interesting prospect he'd
ever encountered.

Except for Cleo North.

Ordinarily Cleo dropped off to sleep five seconds after her
head hit the pillow. Other than Rosie, not too many things
could keep Cleo awake when it was time to sleep, not even
her concerns for the ranch.

But tonight her eyes wouldn't stay closed, and the most
vexing restlessness kept her body from relaxing. She threw
her legs out of the covers, then drew them back. Her arms
wouldn't stay still and first went above her head, then down
to her sides. She turned to one side, then the other, and finally, after a good thirty minutes of rolling around, Cleo
gave up and got out of bed.

Wrapping a robe around herself, she went to the kitchen
and snapped on the light. The small house was silent. Rosie
was asleep in her tiny bedroom, so Cleo very quietly put the
teakettle on the stove to heat.

Leaning against the counter with her arms folded to wait
for the water to boil, Cleo faced what had been brewing
since Chance Saxon's arrival. The man bothered her on a
level she'd thought she was long past ever experiencing
again. For years now, certainly since the months before
Rosie's birth, Cleo hadn't been attracted to one single man.
Nor had she missed having a man in her personal life. To the
contrary, she'd been happy and contented, especially with
her work on the Kidd River Ranch.

Chance was a disturbing distraction. Good-looking men had come along before, and Cleo had had no trouble in refusing whatever they'd hinted at or boldly suggested. But those men hadn't touched her inner self in any way, and Chance Saxon did.

Everything was suddenly at risk, she realized uneasily—her way of life, Rosie's future, her own peace of mind—merely because of another too smooth, too handsome, too sexy man. Her choices were unnerving: Either stay on the ranch and learn to live with simmering sexuality, or leave.

But where would she go? Moving Rosie to a city and working at an ordinary job would mean putting her daughter in someone else's care. Cleo suspected that Rosie was more self-sufficient than the average eight-year-old, but that was out here, where everything was easygoing and familiar to the child. Not for a minute could Cleo leave Rosie alone in strange surroundings, among strange people. Not that Rosie didn't get along with people. The little girl was friendly and completely trusting of everyone she met, although she had been taught in school that not everyone deserved a child's trust. It was just that Rosie hadn't yet met anyone who wasn't kind and good to her.

Cleo realized her fears were those of a mother who had reared her child with constant and abiding love. Never had she raised her voice to Rosie, let alone her hand. Visualizing her little daughter on the streets of some town or city while her mother was at work unnerved Cleo.

When the kettle sang Cleo prepared a cup of tea, which she brought to the table to drink. Her thoughts went back in time, to herself at nine, only one year older than Rosie was now. Her father simply disappeared. There'd been fights between him and Cleo's mother, but suddenly he was gone, without explanation or apology. Cleo had never seen him again.

In the very next year, she lost her mother to a heart ailment. Orphaned, her mother's sister, Mary, and Mary's husband, Ed Graves, packed her things and took her to their ranch. Or what Cleo believed was their ranch. It wasn't un-

til her teens that she learned the land and buildings were
leased by her aunt and uncle.

They hadn't been unkind to her. Childless themselves,
however, they had molded her to fit into their lives, not the
other way around. And they hadn't requested love from her
or offered it. All of her affection went to the ranch, to the
horses, to the land.

When she was eighteen, Ed was killed in a truck accident. The lease was dissolved almost immediately by the
ranch's owners, and Mary and Cleo moved to Billings.
There was enough money for Cleo to attend classes at the
community college, and she took as many business courses
as she could handle while working at a part-time job in a
fast-food restaurant.

To that point, Cleo's interaction with men consisted solely
of dates for high school proms and sporting events. She was
completely unprepared for a man like Jake Hanover, who
was as smooth as they came and handsome enough to be in
the movies. Jake was a superintendent for a highway construction company, and often stopped at the restaurant
where Cleo worked for a quick sandwich.

She noticed him right away, but it wasn't her nature to let
a man know. The problem was, he noticed her, too, and
Jake didn't have a shy hair on his handsome head. When he
asked her out, Cleo's giddiness resulted in an upset stomach. But she went and fell madly in love on that very first
date.

A few evenings later Jake confessed love, as well, and
Cleo believed him with all her heart. He led her into mak-
ing love as easily as a cowpoke led a thirsty horse to water.
She could refuse him nothing and, in truth, didn't even try.

Four weeks later Cleo was walking on air and dreaming
about marriage with her beautiful Jake. Aunt Mary was
ailing, but kept the awful truth of her fatal condition to
herself, which was her nature. When Cleo missed a period,
it startled but didn't frighten her, and she told Jake about it
immediately.

He paled, she remembered now. He got ashy and wouldn't look her in the eye. And then he said the lethal words. "Cleo, I'm already married. You'll have to get an abortion."

Her love died a quick and sudden death at that moment. Cleo was suddenly an adult and she spoke very coldly. "Where's your wife?"

"In California."

"Do you have children?"

"Three. Cleo, will you have an abortion?"

"Yes," she lied.

She never saw Jake again after that evening. He left the area, and Cleo figured he went back to California and his family. He didn't know about Rosie and he never would if she had anything to say about it.

But there was Rosie's future to consider, Cleo knew. She had told Rosie the truth when the little girl asked about her daddy, or as much as a child could digest. "Your daddy and I were never married, sweetheart."

"But where is he, Mama?"

"I suspect he lives in California, but I don't know where."

Someday Rosie might need to know more about her father. She might even be driven to find him, Cleo realized. If and when that day came, she would tell Rosie about Jake's wife and other children.

But she prayed Rosie would never ask.

Aunt Mary had died shortly after Rosie's birth. Alone with a child to raise, Cleo quit school and went to work full-time. Landing her job on the Kidd River Ranch had been her greatest achievement, she firmly believed, other than Rosie. And giving it up because Chance Saxon reminded her of Jake was no small decision. But dear God, why was she destined to get weak-kneed over black hair and blue eyes on a man? To be attracted to polish and confidence and a swaggering walk?

"It isn't fair," Cleo muttered while carrying her empty teacup to the sink. Switching off the kitchen light, she felt her way in the dark to her bedroom.

But instead of disrobing and returning to bed, she went to the window and moved the curtain aside to see out. There was a light on in the big house, in Chance's upstairs bedroom.

He must still be studying those reports, she thought. How strange to have someone living in the big house, to visualize him poring over reports, and trying to get his bearings with the ranch. She had hoped someone from back East would do something about the place, but this scenario had never occurred to her.

Particularly, she never could have imagined the ranch's benefactor creating such disturbance in herself. Or causing her to dredge up the past and worry about the future.

With a heavy sigh, she dropped the curtain, shed her robe and crawled into bed.

Three

Awake and out of bed at 5:30 a.m., Chance stood at the open window of his room and breathed in the fresh morning air. Chance had slept well and felt alive and invigorated. He could see for miles, and the vastness of the country beyond the compound seemed to swell his own soul. The mountains were tinged with the gold of the rising sun and looked glorious.

Hearing voices, he dropped his gaze to see Cleo and Pete talking near the corral. Chance spotted Rosie leaving her house, and then carefully closing the gate in the picket fence. Her two dogs, shut up in the yard, longingly watched their young mistress walking away by peering through the spaces between the pickets.

Chance chuckled softly. He wasn't used to this sort of homey scene, but it gave him a good feeling. Apparently Rosie would accompany him and Cleo on their ride this morning, which was fine with him. But what was wrong with those two pooches tagging along?

He left the window and finished dressing, tugging on boots, slipping into a plain blue shirt and tucking it into his jeans. Cleo was wearing her hat, he'd noticed, so he dug out one of his own. His suitcases were only partially unpacked as he couldn't see any sensible reason for crowding the one modest closet in his room with suits and dinner jackets he wouldn't be wearing. Of course, he could use a closet in one of the other bedrooms, which he'd probably do one of these days as the clothes he had now were apt to be the last expensive garments of his life.

That thought, too, created a chuckle, and he marveled at his own good mood. There was little here to laugh about, certainly not the minuscule balance showing in the checkbook.

His mood remained upbeat, however. Downstairs he greeted Joe with a grin. " 'Morning, Joe.''

Joe gave him a wry nod. ''Breakfast's almost ready. Help yourself to coffee.''

''Thanks, I'll do that.''

Chance filled a thick, graceless mug from the pot on the stove. ''How'd you get into cooking, Joe?''

''Got the rhumatiz and couldn't work out in the weather no more. Cooking's the only thing I know aside of cowboyin'.''

''Cooking is a respectable profession,'' Chance remarked.

''Respectable or not, it's what I do.'' Joe flipped some hotcakes onto a plate. ''Not many folks around to appreciate it anymore, though. Used to be a full table at every settin' in this house.''

''Have you been here very long?''

''Since before the Saxons owned the place. Siddown and eat.''

''Thanks.''

''Yep,'' Joe continued as Chance poured syrup on his pancakes. ''I was tendin' cattle in those days, though.''

"Ever do any ramrodding, Joe?" Chance asked casually, wondering if he hadn't found another brain besides Cleo's to pick.

"Nope. Going riding this mornin'?"

"With Cleo."

"Rosie'll go along, too, you know."

Chance nodded. "I like kids."

"Shucks, Rosie wouldn't be a problem even if you didn't cotton to younguns. Don't even know she's around half the time. Best li'l ol' kid you'd ever hope to meet."

Pete came in, and Joe went to the stove for another batch of pancakes. "'Morning, Chance," Pete said as he hung his hat on a wall hook near the door and took his seat at the table.

Chance figured Pete for around fifty years of age. "Good morning, Pete."

"Joe, you and me are going to Helena this morning," Pete announced.

"What in heck for?" Joe questioned irascibly.

"To return Chance's rental car to the airport."

"Hell's bells," Joe muttered. "Don't like goin' to town and Cleo knows it."

"Well, it's gonna take both of us," Pete retorted. "And those are Cleo's orders."

Chance smiled to himself as the crusty debate went on. When he was finished with breakfast, he put on his hat and went outside, leaving the men to their spirited discussion on which pickup should be the second vehicle for the trip to Helena, Joe's or Pete's.

The clean, clear air seemed to bring the mountains close enough to touch. Chance stood near the house for a moment to drink in the view and marvel again at his own high spirits this morning. Last night he had made a decision: Some of the cattle had to be sold. Not many, certainly no more than were necessary to see him through this first cash crunch. He wasn't worry-free, or shouldn't be, but he still felt like a million bucks. Amazing.

Grinning at nothing in particular, he headed for the barn and corral. On impulse, he veered to Cleo's little house to see Rosie's two dogs up close.

The pair came to the front fence at once and nearly turned inside-out welcoming him. Hunkering down, Chance rubbed their noses through the pickets. "Hey, fellas. Let's see what we can do about setting you free, okay? No reason for two fine dogs like yourselves to be confined to one small space with so much land to explore."

The two tan dogs bounced around and grinned, tumbling over each other to lick Chance's hand. Laughing, he stood up, and spotted Cleo walking toward him.

"Good morning," he called.

"'Morning, Mr. Saxon."

"Hey, none of that today, all right?" But when Cleo got closer, he felt yesterday's emotions all over again. Heaven knew she wasn't dressed or primped to lure a man into anything. Her clothing wasn't any more seductive than his own, old jeans, another plaid cotton shirt, worn boots and that ancient hat.

But her green eyes were bright and brimming with health and vitality. Cleo was like this country, Chance thought, clean and beautiful to the eye, soothing to the soul.

She saw the sparkle in Chance's eyes and relaxed because yesterday's sensuality was absent. "The horses are saddled and ready to go."

"Mine, too?" Chance questioned.

"Why...yes." She had picked a gentle mare for Chance to ride and now wondered if she hadn't presumed too much. "If you don't like her, it will only take a few minutes to..."

"We'll see," Chance said as they started walking toward the barn. He smiled at his companion. "Beautiful morning."

"Yes, but there's some weather on the way. Rain is predicted for this afternoon. We should be back before it hits, though."

They reached the three saddled horses and Rosie, who presented a shy smile. "This is my daughter. Rosie, say hello to Mr. Saxon."

"Hello, Mr. Saxon."

"Hello, Rosie. I stopped by your house to see your dogs. What's their names?"

"Tisk and Task," the youngster replied, drawing a laugh from Chance. "Mama got them for me when they were puppies, and she said they were scoundrels," the child explained.

Cleo laughed, as well. "They were, believe me," she said to Chance. "But they're better behaved now and are good company for Rosie."

"Do you always keep them inside your fence?" Chance asked.

"They can be pesky," Cleo warned, understanding his meaning.

"But what could they hurt?"

"It isn't a matter of them hurting something, Chance."

His gaze connected with hers. "I guarantee they wouldn't bother me, Cleo." His voice became lower, for her ears alone. Rosie was checking the cinch belt on one of the horses and paying no attention. "Set them free. Give them the run of the place. I don't like seeing animals penned up. Never did like zoos for that reason."

Something flowered in Cleo. "I feel the same way. Thank you." She looked at her daughter. "Rosie, run back to the house and open the gate, honey."

Rosie's big blue eyes got bigger. "How come, Mama?"

"Mr. Saxon doesn't want Tisk and Task locked in."

"But they'll run all over the place, Mama. You always said they would be a nuisance to the other people on the ranch."

"Apparently Mr. Saxon feels otherwise."

A slow smile lit Rosie's features and she took off running. Chance realized she had his coloring. Her hair wasn't quite as dark as his, but her eyes were certainly as blue. She was dressed like her mother, though her hat was hanging down her back from a string around her neck. She was a pretty child, and young enough to be his. The notion was startling to Chance, because if there was one aspect of life he'd given little or no thought to, it was having his own children.

"You made her day," Cleo said with a smile.

"What would it take to make yours?" Chance asked softly.

Cleo's smile faded. "Take a look at that gray mare," she said coolly. "If she doesn't suit you, we'll saddle a horse that does."

Chance wouldn't release her gaze. "She'll do for today. I'll look over the stock later on when I have the time. Cleo, don't be afraid of me."

"I'm not afraid of you," she lied.

"Your guard is a foot thick around me."

"You agreed to keeping our relationship impersonal," she reminded him sharply.

Chance looked away. "Yeah, guess I did." He saw what was happening across the compound. "Hey, look at that."

Cleo turned and couldn't help laughing. Tisk and Task were bounding this way and that outside the fence, sniffing everything, yapping eagerly. Rosie came running back. "They're excited!" she yelled. Stopping next to her mother, she said, "Thanks, Mr. Saxon."

"You're welcome, Rosie. And if your mom doesn't mind, I'd like you to call me Chance."

Rosie looked to her mother. "Is it all right, Mama?"

Cleo wasn't thrilled with this unexpected informality. "I . . . suppose so," she said with obvious reluctance.

Chance didn't let it bother him. "Which horse is yours, Rosie?" he asked while moving to the trio of saddled animals.

"The pinto."

He'd expected that reply, as the pinto was the smallest of the horses. "Which means," he said to Cleo. "This big black fellow is yours."

"He really is mine," Cleo explained. "I bought him from a neighboring rancher two years ago."

Chance ran his hand down the horse's left foreleg. "Fine animal. Good legs."

His manner was that of a man who knew horses. Questions suddenly besieged Cleo, about his past, what he'd been doing all his life, and how he felt now without money when he was accustomed to having it. But she kept the sudden curiosity bottled inside her. "Shall we go?"

"I'm ready," Chance agreed.

They mounted and settled into their saddles. Riding away from the buildings with the reins in his hand, Chance felt a song in his heart. This was life at its best, fabulous scenery, clean air and good companions. Even the less than notable mare beneath him seemed great.

"Do these horses have names?" he asked.

"Yours is Pearly, Rosie's is Patches and mine is Midnight."

"Well, Pearly." Chance laughed with a pat to his horse's neck. "Guess we'll get along all right."

Indeed, Chance Saxon had ridden before, Cleo noted. He rode, in fact, with the lazy grace of a lifetime horse lover. For some reason that bit of knowledge warmed her.

But each small step toward emotional closeness made Chance more dangerous to a woman of her determination. They were very different people. Regardless of Chance's present financial difficulties, he'd been raised with wealth. Every dollar Cleo had seen in her entire life had been earned through hard work.

She listened while Chance talked to Rosie, asking her which grade she would enter in the fall, and how she liked her school. Cleo nearly burst with pride in her daughter's ability to converse with an adult of short acquaintance.

Tisk and Task followed for a while, Cleo saw, but then they ran back to the compound, obviously not all that confident with their newly found freedom.

"Chance, your land goes to that dark ridge on the mountain." Cleo pointed it out. "It extends to about a mile beyond the river to the south and takes in those two hills you can see to the north. Its eastern boundary is Nettleton Road, which was the second road you traveled from the highway."

"My land," Chance murmured as Cleo's words sank in. He hadn't really thought of the Kidd River Ranch in that precise terminology before. Of course, Cash and Rush had as much ownership in the place as he did, just as he owned a third of the Nevada and Oregon businesses.

But the land he was riding on was his, and he realized that he had never possessed anything that gave him the same depth of satisfaction he was feeling now. What had he possessed, though? The big luxurious house he'd thought of as home, the yacht, the polo ponies and everything else he'd grown up with had been his grandfather's. As this land had been. Dear God, he'd never owned anything. Even the clothes on his back had been bought with Granddad's money.

A shameful feeling of such magnitude hit Chance, that he actually swayed in the saddle. Why in God's name had he never realized what a parasite he'd been? Why hadn't Granddad said it just once?

Memories flooded Chance's brain and for the first time he saw everything clearly: Granddad had tried to make up for the loss of his grandsons' parents by indulging their smallest whim. He'd literally loved them into uselessness.

Chance couldn't fault his grandfather for neither attitude nor actions, and shied away from anything negative concerning the old gentleman. But it was a damned shame that it took his death and the almost complete destruction of his financial empire to make his grandsons see the light.

At least Chance *hoped* his brothers were undergoing the same metamorphosis as himself.

Cleo and Rosie were riding a little ahead of him, he realized, as though suddenly coming out of a daze. He looked at mother and daughter, so alike in bone structure from behind. Rosie might not have her mother's coloring, but the little girl certainly had her build. Or would have when she reached maturity. And Rosie was a rider, all right, just as Cleo had said. The child's posture was as relaxed as his own, and in truth, she looked like a very tiny adult on that pretty pinto pony.

"There," Cleo said while pointing ahead. She swiveled in the saddle. "Can you see the herd, Chance?"

His eyes adjusted to the distance as he picked out the dots of cattle that were strung along a series of hills. "I see them."

"Can I ride ahead, Mama?" Rosie asked.

"*May* I ride ahead, and yes you may." Cleo smiled. Rosie had an awful time with may and can. The pinto took off, and Chance laughed when the little girl leaned forward and threw her whole body into the gallop.

"She sure can ride," he commented, nudging his horse forward to come abreast of Cleo's Midnight.

"Rosie was only three when we moved out here. I put her on a horse within the week. Needless to say, she loved it immediately."

"Like mother, like daughter?"

"Very much," Cleo concurred.

"She seems like a great kid, Cleo."

"She is."

There'd been no hesitation in Cleo's reply. The hesitation came from Chance as he privately recalled his own childhood. Though he seldom talked about it, especially to someone of short acquaintance, he heard himself saying, "I lost both parents when I was five. They were killed in a plane crash."

The information, coming out of the blue, shocked Cleo. The look she bestowed on her companion was genuinely sympathetic. "I'm sorry."

"Thanks. My brothers and I were well cared for. Our grandfather took us in. What about you, Cleo? Are your parents living?" Who did she have, other than Rosie?

Cleo gave her head a small shake. "My mother's dead. I don't know about my father. He walked out when I was nine and I never saw him again." She glanced again at Chance, uneasily, because she was never comfortable during this sort of personal conversation. Quickly she added, to forestall further questions about her past, "An aunt and uncle raised me."

The somber subject cast a pall on the day, which disturbed Chance. He dropped it at once. "Cleo, I've decided to sell some of the herd."

This topic was more disturbing for Cleo than the previous one. She frowned. "I wish there were another way."

"So do I, but we can build the herd again."

"Natural accretion is a very gradual process."

Chance looked at her. "Wouldn't we double the herd each year?"

"I'm afraid it's not that cut-and-dried." Cleo began an explanation that encompassed stillbirths, weak animals and the customary practice of selling the steers, the castrated male cattle, in the fall of the year. Chance listened, fascinated by Cleo's extensive knowledge of bovine husbandry and, more simply, the business of running a cattle ranch.

They approached the grazing animals; most had white faces though their hides were either black or reddish-brown. "What breed are they?" Chance questioned.

"Mostly Hereford, though there's some Angus blood, as well. They're good stock, Chance, strong and hardy."

They were on the lower rise of the mountain. Chance looked back at the ranch buildings, seeing the swells and dips of the miles of grassland and feeling again the pride of possession. Any opinion could be premature at this point, he knew. He'd been here less than twenty-four hours, after all. But this morning he felt optimistic and excited, and behind the more obvious responses to his new home lay a surprising idea. A man could happily and contentedly live his life out on this fertile and beautiful land.

It was an astonishing theory for a man who was used to having only the very best from whatever whim required pampering. But then, Chance decided, maybe he'd been badly mistaken about what elements constituted the "best" in life.

His gaze returned to Cleo. "This place gets in your blood very quickly, doesn't it?"

She cast him a dubious glance. "It did with me."

"But you have doubts about me."

"I grew up in this environment, Chance. It's very new to you."

He understood what she hadn't said. "You're thinking I won't last, aren't you?"

That was exactly what she'd been thinking, but Cleo only said, "I'd rather not make any such judgments, if you don't mind." She turned her head to see where Rosie was riding.

"Tell me what you're thinking, Cleo," Chance persisted.

She faced him again. "Why?"

"Because you're my link to the place. I admire your grasp of the business, your knowledge. You know every inch of this land, don't you?"

"Yes, and I'm happy to pass on each and every fact I know about the ranch to anyone who's interested. In this case, you. But bringing personal opinions into the picture would probably cause . . . dissension."

Chance shaped a tentative smile. "Dissension is the last thing I want with you, Cleo. I need you."

Cleo's breath caught in her throat. He was talking about the ranch, but implying much more. Or was he? An unfamiliar confusion suddenly muddled her thoughts. For eight years, since before Rosie's birth, Cleo hadn't noticed even one brief moment of confusion around men, and the sensation now angered her.

She swallowed and managed to contain the backlash of temper in her system. "Maybe you'd like to see the river up close. Rosie, we're riding to the river," she called without waiting for Chance's response.

Cleo rode ahead without concerning herself about Chance's compliance. She didn't like what was happening and found it difficult to pretend otherwise. He *wouldn't* last, dammit! Today the scenery and perfect weather awed him, but the novelty was bound to wear off, and then what would happen to the ranch? Even more disturbing, what would happen to her and Rosie if she was stupid enough to fall for another too-sexy, unscrupulous guy?

Not that Chance Saxon's scruples were all that clear to her. But how could she put her trust in a man who was here under duress and probably had never done a lick of real work in his life?

Chance held back and waited for Rosie to catch up. "We're going to the river?" she questioned.

"Your mother suggested I see it up close," Chance explained.

"It's pretty. And you know what? Sometimes Mama lets me swim in it. Only in a few spots, though. Where the water isn't too deep."

"Are you a good swimmer?"

"Not very. I can dog-paddle, though. A little."

"Maybe we can go swimming one of these days and I'll teach you the crawl. That's the overhand stroke."

"Would you really? That'd be great. Mama isn't a very good swimmer, either."

Chance regarded the woman ahead of them, her back board straight, the set of her shoulders conveying her pique. "Maybe I can teach her a few things, too," he said softly, and then smiled at Rosie. "About swimming."

"Thanks, Mr. Saxon."

"Chance, remember?"

"Oh, yeah. Thanks, Chance."

They rode in silence until Rosie asked with a shy sideways glance, "Do you have a little girl, Chance?"

"No, honey." He looked at the small girl riding next to him. "I haven't been that lucky."

Luck wasn't a topic Chance had ever spent much time on. He wasn't a gambler and everything had always come so easy, he'd never had any reason to hope Lady Luck would smile on him. Until recently.

But Cleo was "lucky," and in a way he never could have imagined before this. Her roots went deep and sure, even though buried in another person's land. Her needs were simple: a small house, a steady job and her daughter. He

was complicating her life, Chance knew, which was why she
froze and stiffened every time he inched across that line di-
viding employer and employee.

And "inch" was all he'd done. Barely that. He'd never
been tongue-tied around women and probably never would
be. A personal relationship with Cleo would also compli-
cate *his* life, but knowing that as surely as he knew his own
name didn't seem to have the power to stop him from letting her know he was interested.

He liked her, he liked Rosie. In Cleo's case, the "liking"
went bone-deep. His body stirred at the slightest thought of
sex. The way she rode a horse stirred him, her green eyes
stirred him, her voice, the damned leather gloves on her
hands, the scuffed boots on her feet. A few weeks of this
and he'd probably be salivating at the mere sight of her.

He'd never been so blasted by a woman before. Yesterday he hadn't known she was alive, and today his imagination had gone crazy. It was too soon, too quick. Cleo was
right and he was wrong. Dead wrong.

Determined again to keep his distance, Chance clenched
his jaw. Rosie, he noticed, was humming under her breath,
a pleasant, lulling sound. She was a sweet child, and her
question about him having a little girl gnawed at Chance's
interior. She had to wonder about her father, where he was,
who he was. What did Cleo tell her? Dammit, what could
Cleo tell *him?*

She had to have been in love with the guy or there
wouldn't have been a Rosie. What had he done, taken off
and deserted her as her father had? Or had the man wanted
to marry her and Cleo had refused? Chance couldn't dis-
card that notion merely as a matter of course. Cleo was
strong-minded enough to do exactly that if she'd thought it
best at the time.

And taking a job on a ranch, a *man's* job, for God's sake,
so her young daughter wouldn't be reared by baby-sitters,
evidenced an iron will. Cleo North was no pushover, which
pleased Chance the more he thought about it. Easy women

were no challenge, and he'd never been attracted to "easy."
Maybe that was part of Cleo's big draw, he mused.

Whatever, he was going to stick to his guns this time. No
more flirtatious remarks, no more innuendo. Cleo might not
be easy, but neither was this ranch. And he was going to
make it a success or die trying.

Cleo was wrong about one thing. He was here to stay.

Four

Within three days Chance had arranged transportation to haul fifty head of cattle to auction, which he figured would raise enough cash to see the ranch through the summer. Pete, Cleo, Rosie and Chance rode out to the foothills to cut the fifty head from the herd and then drive them to lower ground. The trucks would pick up the animals at a loading chute located near Nettleton Road.

Cutting and driving cattle was hard work, Chance discovered, though the cutting was harder than the driving. Decisions had to be made about which animals should be sold, and repeatedly he asked, "How about that one?" and Cleo would shake her head. "She throws strong calves."

Finally, fifty head were rounded up and headed toward the compound. "Do you actually know the history of every animal on the place?" Chance questioned Cleo teasingly as they rode along behind the herd.

"Pretty much," Cleo replied evenly.

"Amazing."

"Sensible," Cleo amended. "Some cow ranchers are relying on computers to keep track of breeding records."

"Would you like to have a computer?"

"I don't know a whole lot about them," Cleo admitted. "But the larger the herd, the more sense a computer makes."

"It's an idea to keep in mind for the future."

Every time Chance referred to the future, something in Cleo rebelled. She didn't want to feel that way, but she just couldn't muster any faith in his longevity. Granted, he'd been working hard, getting up early, following either her or Pete and diving into whatever chores were scheduled for the day. Neither could she doubt Chance's intelligence. He soaked up information and exhausted subjects with pertinent, persistent questions. But believing unconditionally that he would be here next month, let alone next year or five years down the road, just wasn't possible for her.

Along with that seemingly immovable opinion was Cleo's awareness of her employer as a man. His good looks were growing on her, his smile and white teeth, his long, lean build, even the way he wore ordinary, everyday clothing. She knew she was functioning on two different levels, Cleo the ranch hand, and Cleo the woman. It was the feminine side of herself that worried her, and the one she vowed to keep hidden from everyone's eyes. Especially Chance's.

By the time the slow-moving procession reached the compound, it was late afternoon. Chance urged his horse closer to Cleo's. "Joe mentioned making a big pot of stew today. Why don't you and Rosie have supper with us?"

Cleo took a second to consider the invitation. She was tired and so was Rosie. After baths, sitting down to a meal of Joe's good cooking was hard to pass up, although she preferred giving Rosie her best efforts at a normal life-style, which to Cleo meant having meals in their own home.

"Thanks," she said. "I'd like that tonight."

Pleased with her acceptance, Chance nudged his horse to take off after a wandering cow. Lightning's quick response was gratifying. Chance had inspected every horse on the place and had chosen a roan gelding for his use. "Lightning" wasn't precisely the roan's speed, but that was his name and Chance had already become fond of the horse.

They stopped the small herd a quarter-mile east of the buildings, a location that would require little time to move the cattle to the loading chute in the morning. The herd milled around a bit, then began grazing. Chance grinned; he'd just been on his first cattle drive.

Pete yelled "Ya-hoo" and began running his horse back to the compound. Rosie took up the race. Cleo laughed, and Chance found himself laughing with her.

"Rosie's always hoping her pinto will beat Pete's quarter horse, but it never will," Cleo explained as she and Chance started back, walking their horses. "Are you familiar with quarter horses? They have tremendous sprinting speed. Pete's horse would give any breed a run for its money up to a quarter of a mile."

They talked about horses during the ride back, lauding the characteristics of different breeds. Chance mentioned the Arabian stock that had been a part of the Saxon stables, and Cleo told him there was a well-known Arabian horse ranch in southeast Montana.

Their conversation was easy and amiable, and Chance didn't miss how well they got along with impersonal topics. He'd been careful lately, choosing his words, making sure he didn't unsettle Cleo with remarks that could be interpreted as intimate. But he thought them; how could he not when he admired her in so many ways? Cleo wasn't the most beautiful woman he'd known, but there was a depth to her beauty he'd never before noticed in a woman. Her strong-mindedness was unquestionable, and Chance was positively enthralled with the relationship between her and Rosie. Cleo never spoke sharply to her daughter, never with condescension or parental upper-handedness. And yet Cleo was in control, very obviously the mother and Rosie, the child. In a way foreign to his experience, Chance ached for Cleo, maybe because she was so adamantly opposed to the passion he felt simmering between them.

Rosie had already unsaddled her pinto and was rubbing the horse down when her mother and Chance rode up.

"Did you win the race?" Cleo asked.

"Not today," Rosie declared in a tone that implied she would try again.

Chance dismounted with a self-satisfied grin. He had enjoyed the day, hard work and all. Cleo and Rosie were coming to the big house for supper. The world seemed pretty much okay right now.

After the animals were tended, everyone went their separate ways, Cleo and Rosie to their house, Pete to the bunkhouse and Chance to the main house. Chance took a hot shower, shaved and put on clean clothes. Then he went down to the study to phone his brothers, first Rush in Nevada then Cash in Oregon.

Like him, they were having their troubles. But he heard in their voices the same thing he'd been feeling—the excitement of self-sufficiency. With the calls completed, he sat back and pondered the transformations taking place with the Saxon brothers. Pride swelled his chest. Their drastic change of financial status had been a setback, not a defeat.

Elated, Chance bounded to his feet. He was ravenously hungry and eager for supper.

Cleo fixed the pink plastic clip in Rosie's dark curls. "There, all done." Rosie was wearing her favorite outfit— a pink jumper and a white T-shirt with a trailing design of pink flowers around the neck and sleeves. "You look very pretty."

"So do you, Mama."

A slight flush tinted Cleo's cheeks. Her simple skirt and blouse couldn't possibly be construed as seductive, but it was feminine. Rosie had seen the invitation to supper in the big house as a special event, and Cleo didn't have the heart to tell her it wasn't. Instead, she'd gone along with Rosie's high spirits and even used a little makeup. If Chance got ideas from a skirt and lipstick, Cleo planned to set him straight, though she didn't relish the prospect and hoped he wouldn't notice.

With her hair done, Rosie began dancing around, singing in her sweet, high voice, "Chance asked us to supper. Chance asked us to supper."

"You like him, don't you?" Cleo asked casually.

Rosie grinned from ear to ear. "He's nice. Don't you think so, Mama? Don't you think Chance is nice?"

"He's...yes, he's a nice man," Cleo allowed. He was particularly nice to Rosie. Effortlessly, too, as though he truly enjoyed talking with her. And, of all things, he was also nice to Tisk and Task, who were becoming rather independent with their recently gained freedom.

Cleo sighed to herself. If a woman wasn't careful, she could fall very hard for Chance Saxon. Certainly, Cleo thought, if she hadn't already experienced a hit-and-run man, she would be in grave danger of liking Chance too much. Rosie's obvious fondness of him nudged Cleo's maternal protectiveness. The little girl was bound to miss having a father, even if she never said so. But focusing her wish for a father, subconsciously or otherwise, on Chance could leave Rosie feeling terribly lost should he just up and desert the ranch one day.

By the time Cleo and Rosie walked to the main house, Cleo was feeling tense. The situation at the Kidd River Ranch looked just fine on the surface, but there were disturbing elements brewing that would bother any thinking woman and mother.

Still, leaving a job she loved and the only home Rosie could remember was Cleo's one alternative to sticking it out. Her job was in jeopardy, anyway, she told herself. Should Chance take a notion to give up on the ranch, that would be the end of her ambivalence as there wouldn't be a job for her or anyone else.

It was better to bide her time and see what happened, she reasoned, arriving at that conclusion just as she and Rosie entered the house.

* * *

During supper Chance remembered his promise to take
Rosie swimming and teach her the crawl. He nearly mentioned it, then decided to discuss it first with Cleo.

She looked so pretty with her hair down and lipstick on
her sensuous mouth, he found himself staring a little too
much. It was apparent, from Cleo's avoidance of direct eye
contact while they ate, that she knew he liked what she'd
done to herself.

Joe served a hearty meal of beef stew, fresh homemade
bread and peach cobbler. Table conversation consisted of
ranch-related topics, and everyone stuffed themselves with
the good food. When they were finished, Pete went outside
to smoke and Joe began clearing away the dishes. From past
experience, Cleo knew Joe didn't want any help in the
kitchen, so she merely complimented his cooking and, with
Rosie in tow, started to leave.

Chance followed with, "I'll walk you home. There are a
few things I'd like to discuss with you."

The sun was sinking behind the mountains, casting long
shadows and softening the light. Chance had been finding
the summer evenings mellow and pleasant, though he had
been putting them to good use by studying the ranch's records and Cleo's reports. He didn't know what else he could
learn by reading them again, and figured that phase of his
education was pretty much completed.

With Rosie walking between her mother and Chance, they
slowly strolled across the compound toward the small house.
"I'm going to have to make a trip to Helena and the bank,"
Chance said. "My signature isn't on file to sign checks."

Cleo figured that aspect of her job was now in Chance's
hands, which was fine as she wasn't overly fond of paperwork. But the chain of command was switching. For a long
time—three years—she'd been boss on the Kidd River
Ranch. It was second nature for her to make the decisions,
to issue the orders, even though her crew had dwindled to
one middle-aged cowpuncher. For the first time, the full

impact of Chance's arrival and takeover really sank in, and it was a strange sensation.

"Yes, of course," she murmured.

Change gave her a keen-eyed look. "I'd still like you to handle the records, Cleo. It just seems sensible that my name be on the bank account."

"It is," she agreed. "But please don't feel you have to appease my ego by—"

"I'm not appeasing anything," Chance interrupted. Rosie suddenly ran ahead, leaving her mother and Chance behind in favor of a romp with Tisk and Task. Chance stopped Cleo with a hand on her arm. "Your knowledge is invaluable, Cleo. If you walked away from this place tomorrow, I'd be in one hell of fix."

Cleo looked into his dark blue eyes and took a slow breath. "I really don't think so. You're much more capable out here than you realize."

Their gazes remained united. "But you're not going to walk away, are you?" Chance softly questioned.

The moment had sprung upon them so quickly. One second Rosie had been between them and the next she wasn't. Nothing separated them now but their own wills, and Cleo wondered if hers wasn't disappearing behind the mountains along with the setting sun.

"I told you how I feel about this place," she said in a voice that had become oddly husky.

"Yes, but there've been a lot of changes in your world, Cleo. You're torn between relief that I'm here and fear of a personal involvement." He paused, then added, "Isn't that true?"

"Not fear," she responded in a stronger voice. "Common sense."

"Don't you think I see the snags in a relationship between us as well as you do? I need your ranching experience, Cleo. I'm learning, yes, but it'll be a long while before I can do what you accomplish so easily. I've told myself that same thing a hundred times, but common sense, as you put it, doesn't kill feelings."

She swallowed and tore her gaze from his, looking off into the distance and registering very little of what she was seeing. "What do you want from me?"

Chance frowned. "That's an ugly question."

Her head jerked around. "It's a down-to-earth question!"

"You're as attracted to me as I am to you," Chance accused.

Cleo's eyes flashed. "I will never become involved in another relationship without first looking at it for a good long time."

"You're talking about Rosie's father."

"Maybe I am, but that subject isn't open for discussion."

"Cleo, comparing me to another man isn't fair."

He still had hold of her arm, and Cleo abruptly shook off his hand. "I'll be the judge of that. It's my life, and my daughter's, and—"

Chance cut in. "It's my life, too."

"Yes, but your life could change directions within the next hour!"

Chance stared. "You still think I'm going to just vanish one day."

What Cleo really thought about anything was escaping her. This conversation had arisen so unexpectedly, and she wasn't prepared to blurt out every one of her doubts about Chance. She certainly couldn't do so without tact, for pity's sake. He was still her employer, even if he was willing to risk those "snags" he'd mentioned to have her.

To have her. The phrase felt like a lump of lead in Cleo's stomach, yet it was how she saw Chance's advances. He certainly wasn't thinking of anything else with a countrified woman of her limited sexual experience . . . a man like him? A man who'd probably seen all there was to see of the world and must have known an uncountable number of gorgeous, witty and no doubt wealthy women? No, he wasn't thinking of anything beyond an affair with Cleo North.

She deliberately squared her shoulders and lied. "I'm completely neutral on the subject of your future." After a brief pause, she added, "What you do with your life is your business. And what I do with my life is mine."

Chance's eyes narrowed. "And there's no common ground?"

"I'd say this ranch is common ground. I work here, you own it."

Her cold but accurate assessment of their positions smarted and spoke volumes about her attitude. Chance suddenly wanted to stop talking and kiss her, to pull her up against himself and kiss her until she admitted what he knew was the God's truth. He just might damn the consequences and do it, too, if Rosie wasn't a hundred feet away.

Cleo felt a deeply rooted tremor within herself and wondered how much longer she could stand there with a brave expression. "Is there anything else?" she questioned.

Chance's eyes went to Rosie. "Yeah, there is. I told Rosie I'd teach her how to swim, but..."

"When did you do that?"

Their gazes clashed again. "The day you showed me the herd for the first time. I'd like to keep my word to Rosie, with your permission."

"I...don't know," Cleo hedged, uncertain about this new twist. "I don't like Rosie going near the river without me."

"You're invited, too," Chance said flatly.

"When were you thinking of doing it?"

"Tomorrow after the trucks pick up the cattle."

A momentary relief rippled through Cleo. "She can't tomorrow. She'll be at a friend's house all day and tomorrow night. A birthday-slumber party."

Chance's expression hardened. "Then tomorrow would be a good day for you and I to go to the bank."

"You don't need me going with you." Instantly Cleo realized that he *did* need her going with him. No one in the bank knew him, and since she was the only one presently authorized to sign checks for the ranch, her permission would be required to add a second signatory. She sighed, because there was no getting out of the trip to Helena. "Fine," she said dully. "We'll go tomorrow and get it done."

"Thank you," Chance said with some sarcasm. "Please say good-night to Rosie for me."

Cleo stood there as he walked off, heading back to the main house. She regretted making him angry, but it wasn't possible to maintain her standards and pacify his ego at the same time. Why were things getting so muddled? Why couldn't Chance take care of his wandering libido without involving her? She'd given him no reason to think she was available, unless a simple skirt and a dab of lipstick could be construed as an announcement of availability. Angry, Cleo started for her own house. "Rosie, I'm going in," she called.

"Can... *may* I stay out for a while, Mama?"

In spite of her own dour mood, Cleo spoke calmly. "It'll be dark soon. Only about fifteen minutes, okay?"

"Okay," Rosie agreed. "Where's Chance, Mama?"

"He went in for the night. Be careful with your good clothes, honey." As Cleo went into her house she heard Rosie's giggles and the two dogs' playful yaps.

The interior of the house was quite dark as she hadn't left a light on. Cleo plopped down on a chair in the minuscule living room and brooded about what was happening with Chance and her. When he wasn't attempting to break down her defenses, she liked him. Without the sexual feelings between them, they could work together ad infinitum. But the feelings were there, and what should she do about them? What did she *want* to do?

Cleo slowly dragged air into her lungs as the truth unraveled in her mind. Her way of life was lonely, which she'd never had cause to consider before. Until Chance, no one had come along to make her think about loneliness. Jake had been a cheat and a liar, a wolf in sheep's clothing, but he'd taught her a great deal about human emotion and adult passion, about loving a man, and how a man's desire could make life seem so worthwhile. Since then, she'd distanced herself from every possibility of a repeat of that fiasco, and for the first time such seclusion didn't seem altogether sensible.

Deserting her chair, Cleo paced the darkening house. Chance Saxon wasn't the man for her, that much was certain, but she had to stop discouraging every man who approached her. She was young, not yet thirty, and Chance kept reminding her that she was a woman with as many active hormones as any other. Supposing she could live out her life totally isolated from the opposite sex was shortsighted, though her methods had worked until recently. But it was becoming clearer by the day that she was changing, and so must her attitude toward men.

Rosie ran in. "Mama, it's dark in here."

Cleo snapped on a light and greeted her daughter with a weary smile. "Close the door, honey. It's time to call it a day.

With the semitrucks lumbering off, loaded with bawling cattle, Chance beckoned to Cleo with a gloved hand. "Ready to go to Helena?"

"Whenever you say."

"Pete," Chance called. "Will you take care of our horses? Cleo and I have to leave for Helena."

"Sure thing," Pete agreed.

They dismounted near the barn. "I'll check with Joe to see if he needs me to pick up anything while we're in town," Cleo said.

"I already talked to Joe, and he said he got everything he needed the day he and Pete returned my rental car."

"Oh. Well, fine," Cleo conceded. "I'll wash up and be back in a minute."

Chance went to the main house to wash up, as well. Chores had been light that morning and his clothes hadn't gotten dirty, so he didn't change from his jeans and work shirt. Besides, he didn't plan to dazzle the banker with city clothes. He wanted to show whomever he met today that he was a working rancher, as it had occurred to him that initiating a conversation about the possibility of a loan would be sensible.

Ten minutes later he was outside again, and looking over the ranch's two vehicles. The blue pickup and the black Blazer were years old, which didn't matter, but both were coated with dust inside and out. Chance frowned. If there was anything he abhorred, it was a dirty car, but he didn't want to take time now to wash one of the vehicles. He glanced at Cleo's van, which was almost as shiny-clean as a new penny.

Cleo walked up. "All set."

Chance turned. "Would you mind if we took your van?"

"I wouldn't mind at all," she said simply. "But why? Is there something wrong with the pickup and Blazer?"

"They're filthy."

"Filthy" might have been a mite strong, but there was no question about both rigs needing a wash. Keeping them clean was one of Joe's chores, which Cleo refrained from pointing out. In all that had been going on, she hadn't noticed that Joe had neglected this phase of his duties, nor would she call it to Chance's attention now.

"I'll see that they're washed when we get back," she said instead. "The keys to the van are at the house. I'll go get them."

While she sprinted away, Chance cursed under his breath. He hadn't meant to imply that keeping the vehicles clean was Cleo's duty, though he was fully aware of her strong sense of responsibility and should have foreseen how she would take his dislike of dirty cars.

This lord of the manor role he'd been thrust into had some extremely subtle nuances, Chance thought. Yes, he was accustomed to getting what he wanted with few words, but not with employees.

Cleo returned with the keys. "Would you like to drive?"

"Would you like me to?"

"It's your decision."

So much was his decision these days, from selling some of the cattle to an incident as mundane as this. Realizing that he was beginning to grasp the full scope of his undertaking in Montana, Chance's mouth thinned. "It's your van. You drive."

Cleo shrugged. "Fine." It made no difference to her, and she climbed into the driver's seat while Chance went around the front of the van to the passenger's side.

Settled and headed away from the ranch, Chance remarked, "I saw you and Rosie driving away earlier. Where did you take her?"

"Her little friend lives about fifteen miles to the north. Today is Darcy's birthday. Her father is taking six of her friends on a horseback ride and picnic." Cleo smiled indulgently, fondly. "Those kids have the whole day planned. Horseback ride, picnic lunch, barbecued burgers for supper and a slumber party tonight."

"Rosie will like it, won't she?"

"Rosie is ecstatic," Cleo replied.

"Do you do that sort of thing for her birthday?"

"We always have a party, but Rosie's birthday falls in January so the festivities are mostly indoors."

"Cleo, when I mentioned the dirty vehicles, it wasn't to lay blame on you."

Cleo sent him a glance. "You have the right."

Chance scowled. "You have enough to do without worrying about washing the pickup and Blazer. I'll do it from now on."

"That isn't necessary. I'll see that it's taken care of. No one's been driving the pickup and Blazer very much, and the chore simply got overlooked."

Seeing that she was adamant, Chance changed the subject. "Tell me about the bankers you've been dealing with."

Cleo gave a short laugh. "I haven't been dealing with any bankers. The ranch's deposits are either mailed in or dropped off at the drive-through window. That's been the sum of my association with the Helena bank."

It was food for thought and disturbing. For some reason Chance had visualized an introduction to bank officials today. It was apparent now that any interaction along those lines would have to come directly from him.

Maybe he *should* have worn something besides jeans and boots.

He whiled away the miles in private thoughts. This was a different world than he knew. How was he doing? What was Cleo's opinion of his efforts?

He glanced her way and was instantly shaken by an awareness of their isolation. There wasn't even another car on the road, and away from the ranch like this, there was no one to intrude on anything they might do or say.

Cleo sensed his stare and darted him a look. "Something on your mind?"

"What do you do for fun, Cleo?"

"For fun?" she echoed with some incredulity. "What kind of fun?"

"Amusement, entertainment. There's no television to watch. Do you read? Sew? What, Cleo? Everyone needs something they enjoy doing when their work is done."

"What do you enjoy doing when the work's done?"

"You're evading my question."

"Fun isn't something I waste time worrying about," she replied coolly.

"Do you actually believe a favorite pastime or a hobby is a waste of time?"

The subject was making Cleo uneasy. She never ran out of things to do, but cleaning her house or doing the laundry when her day of work on the ranch was over could hardly be construed as a hobby.

Chance enjoyed so many activities—golf, tennis, skiing, polo, reading, hiking—that he couldn't quite grasp anyone not being passionate about at least one leisure pastime. Granted, Cleo wasn't like anyone else he knew. Take her attitude on men, for instance. Who else that he'd ever met could decide to give up dating and stick to it?

He clamped his lips together to avoid further questions. He hadn't meant to pry with Cleo; his bid to learn what she did for entertainment had been no more than simple curiosity.

But her life-style was damned amazing. Perplexing. If he were to believe what she'd said about not dating, she hadn't slept with a man for how long? Since Rosie's birth? For eight years?

Cleo was driving with her attention riveted on the road. Chance slid his eyes to the left to take a furtive look at her. Did the idea of her prolonged abstinence make her sexier to him? Something made her sexy to him, something powerful and almost merciless in its tenacity. Chemistry, probably; though the very sight of her was provocative. Just looking at her long legs and shiny hair brought a sexual buzz to his system.

It was strange how these things happened, he thought while facing front again, though his own personal experience with instant attraction had been thus far limited to reading about it, or hearing about it from some guy bragging about his sexual prowess. Actually stories of that nature, or novels with wild sex scenes, had never interested him much. His attraction to Cleo wasn't the same thing. This feeling was happening to him and was perturbingly real. Ignoring it was becoming impossible.

But he didn't know how to get past Cleo's objections, especially when he wasn't positive what they were. They had something to do with Rosie's father, of course. But getting down to basics, what did the memory of one man have to do with another one eight years later?

Five

―

"It's past noon. How about some lunch before we start back?" Chance said as they walked out of the bank.

"Sounds good," Cleo agreed. There was a café across the street. "That place looks all right."

"It's fine with me."

They crossed the street, went into the café and sat at a table. Menus were delivered by a waitress who asked brightly, "How are you today?"

"Just fine, thank you," Cleo replied while setting her menu aside. "I'll have a hamburger and coffee."

Chance quickly scanned the available items, then closed his menu. "Make that two of the same."

With the waitress and menus gone, Cleo said, "You did very well with John Holby." She was referring to Chance's impressive and surprising—to her—air of confidence with the banker. Chance had not only introduced himself to Mr. Holby, but he had also laid out, briefly, the ranch's potential and possible need of a loan in the coming months.

"He seems like an all-right guy," Chance said.

"He has a reputation, Chance, for toughness and extreme caution with bank loans."

"But he seemed receptive to the idea, don't you think?"

Cleo nodded, although burdening the Kidd River Ranch with a mortgage was a frightening prospect to her. If there was any other way, any way at all, it would be more appealing than mortgaging the land. She didn't figure it was her place to say so, though.

Chance liked sitting across a small table from Cleo, even if it was in a nondescript little restaurant with a dozen or so other tables crowded with folks talking and laughing their way through lunch. He thought of some of the glamorous cafés and clubs he'd eaten in, and realized that he was perfectly content to be anticipating a cup of coffee and a hamburger with Cleo.

"You know," he said slowly. "There's really no critical reason to hurry home today. What would you say to touring the area before heading back?"

A frisson of excitement walked up Cleo's spine, a sensation she instantly denied. The last thing she needed was an aimless afternoon in Chance's company. "We really should get back, Chance. I have work to do."

He grinned lazily and sat back in his chair. "I'm the boss, and you just got the afternoon off. Providing—" his blue eyes became mischievous "—you use it to show me the sights."

There were plenty of sights to see within a reasonable radius—Flathead Lake with its beautiful lake islands, for instance—but sharing scenery and conversation with Chance for hours on end was a disconcerting prospect.

"Really," she said calmly, her tone in direct opposition to her over-fast pulse beat, "it's a nice idea, but . . ."

"No more arguments," Chance interrupted firmly. "Rosie's in good hands and the ranch won't disintegrate if you're not watching over it for a few hours."

Cleo hadn't expected this from the day, and she became very still while the waitress delivered cups of hot coffee to the table. Chance eyed his forewoman over the rim of his cup while he sipped, recognizing Cleo's uneasy acceptance of his insistence.

But he couldn't muster any regret for using his position to coerce her into a few hours of freedom from responsibility. Today was an unexpected opportunity to spend time alone with her, of which there were blessed few. Never could he resent Cleo's dedication to her daughter, nor to the ranch. But between the little girl and Cleo's duties, Cleo rarely had a minute to call her own.

"Come on," he said in a gentler tone. "It'll be fun."

The word *fun* reminded Cleo of Chance's question about what she did for amusement, and set off an unusual progression of thoughts for the second time that day. The entirety of her existence revolved around her job and Rosie, and had for years. She had no close friends, unless Joe and Pete could be considered as such. Her excursions from the ranch consisted of tasks related to the ranch, or prompted by some need of Rosie's, such as a parent-teacher conference during the school year, or driving Rosie to one little friend or another's home as had occurred this morning. She never gave herself time, consideration or concern, which had seemed perfectly normal for years, and now, out of the blue, didn't.

A burst of resentment struck her, an unfamiliar rebellion aimed at life itself. Jake Hanover had mowed her over with masculine good looks and a lethal charm, the same traits that were sitting across the table from her at this very moment. But she was no longer the naive, trusting girl she'd been then, which Chance had to know from her unyielding attitude.

He wouldn't push her into anything, she thought with a determined glint in her eyes. An afternoon together without the safety of work to buffer emotions was not going to gain him one darned thing.

"All right," she conceded. "Where would you like to go?"

"Nowhere in particular." Chance smiled. "I'd just like to drive around and see a little more of Montana."

The waitress appeared with their food and set plates before them. "Fine," Cleo agreed. "Maybe you'd like to visit Flathead Lake."

"Sure, that'd be great."

Cleo drove, taking a road that went first west and then in a northwesterly direction from Helena. Chance was interested in everything in sight, and Cleo pointed out the Swan Range, the Rattlesnake Mountains and the Mission Range. They passed through small towns and settlements, and traveled long stretches with little traffic and virtually no population.

"Montana's an enormous state," Chance commented.

"A hundred and forty-five thousand square miles."

Chance glanced behind his seat to the van's interior. "This is a nice unit. You even have a refrigerator."

The van was also equipped with a small two-burner propane-gas stove and a large couch that transformed into a bed. "I bought this to take Rosie camping," Cleo explained. "I don't like sleeping on the ground."

Chance grinned. "Then you do have something you enjoy doing during leisure time."

"Yes, I like camping," Cleo concurred.

"But you take the comforts of home with you." Chance chuckled. "I thought you might be one of those people who enjoyed roughing it, Cleo."

She sent him a raised-eyebrow look. "Sorry to disappoint you."

"I'm not disappointed, believe me," Chance said softly while his gaze drifted over her, starting with her sexy mouth and ending with the boots on her feet. When she'd gone to her house to wash up, she had returned without her hat. During the interim she had taken her hair down and brushed it into a smooth frame around her face, securing it at her nape with a tiny piece of black ribbon.

"I've got an idea," he added teasingly. "Why don't you untie that ribbon?"

"What ribbon?" It took a second for Cleo to understand his meaning. Reflexively her hand left the steering wheel and went to the back of her head. But it wasn't to untie the ribbon, but to make sure it was securely in place. "I like my hair back," she said coolly.

"And you *don't* like my idea."

The problem was that she liked his idea a little too much, or some traitorous portion of herself did.

"Take that road," Chance said suddenly.

Cleo stepped on the brake and veered the van to the side of the highway, where she peered at the old road. "I've never been on it. It looks like it goes into the mountains."

"Great. Let's see where it leads."

"I thought you wanted to see the lake."

"I'd rather follow that old road. Come on, Cleo. Where's your sense of adventure?"

There were no signs listing ranches, Cleo noted. No Forest Service notices denoting scenic areas or fishing streams. No county markers, nothing.

"It probably just peters out after a few miles," she said hesitantly. "Maybe there was a ranch out here at one time." Chance said nothing, and after a moment Cleo sighed. "Fine. We'll see where it goes."

The roadbed was hard-packed dirt, little more than a trail across sagey, rather barren land. But it soon headed into the trees and began ascending. The pine forest was cool and shadowed, lovely, and Cleo began relaxing. Regardless of her previous reluctance to follow a completely unknown road, she did have a sense of adventure, and it was beginning to kick in.

Chance's absorption kept him on the edge of his seat. The van was moving slowly, dodging holes and rocks in the crude road. They rounded a curve and two deer darted into the trees, delighting him.

"This is what I enjoyed most in Australia, poking around back roads," Chance said with excitement in his voice.

"You've been to Australia?"

"I spent two months there recently."

"You've been all over the world, haven't you?" Cleo said quietly.

"I've seen a lot of it," Chance admitted. He brought his gaze from the scenery to Cleo. "Have you done any traveling?"

"Been to Billings," Cleo quipped. She took a moment from the road to look at Chance and said less flippantly, "I've been in three states, Wyoming, Idaho and Montana, the total of my travels."

The disparity of their backgrounds gave Chance a start. He'd known it before, of course, but not with such distinction. Maybe, he mused, it was something Cleo couldn't overlook and what kept her so guarded with him.

He wanted to ease her mind about it. "Would you like to travel?"

Cleo shrugged. "Never gave it much thought. Maybe someday." It was true she hadn't given time to such ideas, but she'd been so wrapped up in making a living and a home for her daughter, trips and things she would probably never be able to afford rarely entered her mind. She was a pragmatic person, Cleo knew, doing what had to be done and mostly content with her lot in life. It took a man like Chance to make a woman think of moonlight on the pyramids, or dancing till dawn on a luxury cruise ship.

Those dreams weren't for her. *Her* dreams consisted of a good education for Rosie, and an occasional camping trip to Glacier or Yellowstone National Park.

"Oh, look," she said as the trees suddenly parted. She stopped the van on the edge of a spectacular view. Flathead Lake was in the distance, surrounded by dark green, heavily treed mountains. Several towns could be seen, particularly Polson.

"Let's get out." Chance opened his door.

Cleo cut the engine and got out to stand at the front of the van with Chance. "This is magnificent," he breathed huskily, utterly enthralled with the panorama before them. "Wish I had a camera with me. I'd like to send pictures of this to my brothers."

"You could always come back," Cleo suggested.

Chance nodded. "I'll do it, too." His eyes left the view to look at Cleo. "Will you come back with me?"

It was so quiet. Without the van's engine, the forest was breathtakingly hushed. Cleo had planned to keep the van moving until they returned to the ranch. Driving was safe; this was not.

She turned, intending to put some distance between them. "Where're you going?" Chance stopped her with a hand on her arm. "Don't run away, Cleo."

She wasn't breathing normally. Her chest felt tight and constricted. "Then don't look at me like that."

"I was looking at the view," Chance rebutted softly.

She could have argued the point, but her heart was beating unusually fast and he was much too close. His hand was completely curled around her arm in a confining clasp. She tried to shake it off, as she'd done once before.

Only it wouldn't budge this time. "Chance...please." Her voice surprised her, sounding almost hoarse.

He stared into her eyes. "What are you afraid of?"

"Dammit, we've *had* this conversation!"

"In the middle of the compound." Chance pointed this out gruffly. "We're alone now."

How well she recognized their isolation! Better than him, probably. Outside of her feverish thoughts a bird twittered. A breeze caught a strand of her hair and tossed it along her cheek.

And Chance just kept looking at her, and hanging on to her arm. What was hardest to digest was that she wasn't doing anything about it, not physically, at any rate. Never had a man put his hands on her without her permission. Her nature would have her lighting into anyone who tried anything she didn't want.

But her fighting nature was strangely dormant at the present, in some sort of idling mode as though waiting for instructions from her brain. Cleo found herself looking at Chance's mouth, and had to forcibly stop the foolish whimper welling in her throat.

With his free hand Chance gently brushed the dancing strand of hair from her cheek. "Your eyes are as big as saucers. You know I want to kiss you, don't you?"

"I know," she whispered.

"What do you want?"

"I . . . we can't do this."

"Maybe we shouldn't do it. But there's a world of difference between *shouldn't* and *can't*. Tell me the truth. Aren't you attracted to me?"

The word puffed out of her, as though pushed by a mystical inner force. "Yes."

Chance dropped her arm and brought her forward. The embrace was rough and a little wild. Their lips met in an explosive passion. It was never a simple kiss, never innocent. Instantly they were straining together. His tongue was in her mouth while his hands splayed on her hips and urged her closer.

Dazed, Cleo tried to think, to cling to some small scrap of sanity. But emotions were overwhelming her. Desire, as she'd never imagined, had her kissing him back, feverishly, and hungrily groping for his body.

Her shirt was suddenly unbuttoned and thrust aside, then her bra, and he was kissing and licking her breasts. She moaned when his mouth opened around one and he sucked on the nipple. His hand was between her legs, stroking her through her jeans, and she began doing the same to him, feeling the strength and potency of his arousal beneath the rough denim fabric.

He took her mouth again in a long devouring kiss, and she could barely stand from the trembling of her legs. Time seemed frozen, unimportant. Where they were, who they were, her life, his, were irrelevant. Rosie never entered her mind, nor did the past and her very substantial reason for living without this kind of passion.

As though from miles away she heard the slide and slam of the van's side door as it was pushed open. She was aware of Chance leading her inside, of him laying her on her own couch, but only vaguely. He took off his shirt, his boots and socks, his jeans and underwear, and she merely stared while her head went round and round in a crazy, benumbed circle.

His body was beautiful, powerful, and she couldn't stop looking at him. He lay down next to her and took her into his arms. Breathing hard, his kisses fell on her mouth, her cheeks, her throat, her breasts. She writhed against him, straining for an impossible intimacy with her jeans between them.

But along with her boots, the jeans proved of small importance, because one minute they were there and the next they weren't. Her conscience suddenly stirred, but it was a belated awakening. As though in a trance, she lifted her hips while Chance removed the last of her clothing.

His hot, intense kisses never stopped. His hands never stopped. Each kiss, each caress lifted Cleo higher, brought her closer to the flames. She didn't rise passively. Her hands were as curious, as greedy as Chance's, her kisses every bit as demanding and relentless.

There was no hesitation and very few words. When he was lying on top of her, buried in her, Cleo wrapped her legs around his hips and drew him deeper. The thrusts of his manhood set off fireworks in her body, pinwheels and sparklers that got brighter and larger and more exciting with each movement. There was a husky croon in her throat, a sensual song of approval and encouragement. She rocked with her lover, held him, kissed him, and raked his back with her nails as the pressure began mounting.

They crashed into paradise together, clinging and groaning and making the heart-stopping pleasure last as long as possible.

Stillness descended then, suddenly, abruptly. Their hearts and their breathing began to slow down.

Reality returned to Cleo first. Her more normal heartbeat speeded up again. Her mouth was suddenly dry. There was no escaping what she'd just done. She'd forgotten everything. Rosie. Jake. Her vow to never let it happen again.

To never again be swayed by an overabundance of sex appeal. Panic threatened. They had used no protection!

"Get up," she cried.

"What?" Chance raised his head.

She wanted to call him names, to curse him. Instead she gritted her teeth and moaned, "Get up. Let me up."

Frowning, Chance slid to the narrow bed. It was then that *his* reality returned. He'd lost his head. He'd only meant to kiss her. Just once.

Cleo grabbed her clothes and ducked out of the van. Chance sat up and rubbed his mouth. He'd never gone off the deep end as he'd just done with Cleo, never lost every drop of self-control before. There was no excuse for making love without protection; there were condoms in his wallet.

But she was the wildest, sexiest woman he'd ever gotten near. He swore under his breath and reached for his underwear. Their need of each other had developed at their first meeting and had simmered ever since. Small wonder it had gotten so out of hand at the first opportunity.

He was dressed and standing outside when Cleo returned wearing her clothes. Her face was pale, her hair tangled. Somewhere along the line she'd lost the ribbon from her hair, which was no big mystery. He'd claimed every inch of her, as she'd done with him, roughly, possessively.

Looking at her, Chance realized he'd like to do it all again. He *could* do it all again. His body was gearing up, in fact, for exactly that.

He told his damned libido to cool off, though if Cleo agreed he'd gladly spend the rest of the day right here. "Are you all right?"

She leveled a cold, malicious look on him. "Was that why you insisted we take the van today?"

His eyes narrowed. "No, it wasn't why I *asked* to take your van today. Cleo, I'm sorry about the unnecessary risk. I've got protection in my wallet."

"Wonderful," she said sarcastically. "Obviously you're prepared for idiotic women, but why in hell didn't you use it?"

"You're not an idiot, and I don't know why I didn't use it. You have to admit we were both pretty carried away."

She was furious. "Let's get back to the ranch so I can pack my things and get the hell away from you!"

Startled, Chance watched her slam the side door of the van shut. "Cleo, stop it. There's no reason for you to leave the ranch because of this."

"No reason?" She turned blazing eyes on him. "What's in your scheming mind now, Saxon? Do you actually have the bloody gall to think I'm going to work for you during the day and sneak into your bed at night?"

The idea excited Chance, but he didn't dare say so. "We'll do whatever you say. Make no mistake, I'd repeat today anytime you said the word, but I promise to keep my hands to myself unless you do."

She scoffed. "Yeah, right. Come on, let's go." Storming around the front of the van, Cleo climbed behind the wheel.

Chance got in on his side, but before Cleo could start the engine he yanked the key out of the ignition. "We need to talk about this," he told her when she glared at him. "Cleo, what happened here between us never happened to me before."

"Don't start with a line, for God's sake. I'll never believe you haven't been with hundreds of women."

"Hundreds! Good Lord, what do you think I am? Besides, I didn't mean I was a virgin. I was talking about forgetting everything else." His voice dropped. "You're potent, Cleo. For me, anyway. I knew it the first day I got to the ranch and met you."

She couldn't be kind. "What would you like me to do now, simper and smile and thank you because I affect you?" She held out her hand. "Give me the keys."

"Not until you calm down and talk to me about this sensibly. Cleo, I need you at the ranch and you need the job. You can't uproot Rosie because you're afraid this will happen again. We're both adults. We can see that it *doesn't* happen again if it bothers you so much."

Her expression was truly scathing. "Does the idea of a baby *bother* you in the least? Or are you even aware of what makes babies?"

Chance's eyes darkened. "I didn't force you, Cleo."

"You started it!"

"I only meant to kiss you!"

"You did a hell of a lot more than kiss me!"

"So did you!"

Cleo covered her face with her hands. "Oh, hell." Her hands fell away. "I asked what you wanted from me last night, when we both knew all along what it was." She turned her head slightly to glare at him. "You got exactly what you wanted, but I expect that's par for the course for you."

Chance's anger was gaining momentum. "Didn't you get exactly what you wanted, too? If you didn't, it wasn't because I didn't try to give it to you, baby."

"You bastard. Give me those keys." Cleo lunged across the aisle for them. Chance tossed them out the window and pulled her across his lap. Cleo struggled and laid a few other names on him, but he grabbed her wrists and held her right where she was.

Their faces were an inch apart. Chance's anger evolved to desire very quickly. "Let's make love, not war," he said huskily. "Cleo, I feel something very special for you."

"So did Jake," she said dully.

"Rosie's father? Cleo, I'm not Jake." Remembering Rosie's dark hair and blue eyes, so much like his own, a startling idea came to him. "Do I look like him?"

The fight was draining from Cleo's system. "No," she said wearily. "You don't look like him, but..."

"But he had dark hair and blue eyes and you see similarities." Chance finished her sentence. "What similarities, Cleo? Actions? Gestures? Voices? What?"

"I don't want to talk about it. Will you please let go of my wrists? I don't want to be on your lap like this."

"You can tell I'm aroused again, can't you?" Chance questioned softly.

"It's pretty obvious."

"That's what you do to me, honey." He tried to kiss her, but she turned her face and his mouth landed near her ear. "I won't push you," he whispered. "But even if you leave the ranch, it's not over for us, Cleo."

Cleo stiffened. "You'll never know where I go."

"Yes, I will. Count on it." After a moment, Chance let go of her wrists. "I'd be a happy man if you sat here on your own, Cleo."

She leaped off his lap and to the driver's seat. Sighing, Chance opened his door and got out for the keys.

Forgetting the torrid encounter on the van's couch on that old road wasn't possible for Chance, and when he wasn't trying to cajole Cleo into conversation during the drive home, he was thinking of how she looked naked and flushed, how her mouth felt under his, how her body felt wrapped around his. It was enough, he thought, to give a man a permanent fever.

Today was not something he would easily get over. No man would, not if the lady was in close proximity as he hoped Cleo would be. But he had to convince her it wouldn't happen again. If she packed up Rosie and her possessions and left, his promise to keep track of her wouldn't be worth a whole lot. The world was a big place. Hell, Montana was a big place. If Cleo never stepped foot over the state line he'd have a hard time tracking her if she didn't want to be found.

He put genuine sincerity in his voice, because the thought of her taking Rosie and disappearing was like a blow to the belly.

"Cleo, I'm more sorry than I can say." She sent him an emotionless glance, which raised his hopes. At least she wasn't shooting daggers at him. "Look, I know I promised before to keep things impersonal between us, but this time I swear it."

Packing up and leaving the ranch wasn't as simple as Cleo had made it sound. In the first place, the furniture in the small house was hers, so it wasn't a matter of throwing her and Rosie's clothes in the van and driving off. Besides, where would she go? Jobs for female cowpunchers weren't exactly scattered along the roadside just waiting for someone to come along and scoop them up. She had a few contacts, sure, but locating a new employer would take time.

She slapped the steering wheel, angry again. How could anyone be such a damned fool twice in a lifetime? With her bad luck with men, she was probably pregnant right this minute.

Her furious gaze landed on Chance, and seeing it, he gave her a tentative smile. Her eyes narrowed. "You might not be so quick to smile if . . ." she began, then clamped her lips tightly together.

"If what, Cleo?"

"Nothing," she said flatly.

What had she been on the verge of saying? Frowning, Chance tried to figure it out. He wouldn't be so quick to smile if . . . what happened? She was driving, staring at the road, showing him a rigid profile.

"If you're pregnant?" he said suddenly. "Is that what you were going to say?"

"Don't be absurd," she snapped. But her pulse ran wild.

Chance leaned forward, his gaze intent on the road while he contemplated the possibility. It wasn't likely, he told himself. What were the odds of today—this afternoon—being the brief fertile period in Cleo's monthly cycle?

But supposing the odds were against them and it had happened? What then?

"I wouldn't desert you," he said quietly. "Don't ever think that. I don't know what happened with that Jake character, but . . ."

Cleo had to stop him. His words were clawing at her. She did so by laughing, which startled the somberness out of him. "Is something funny?" he questioned coolly.

"Uh . . . no. But please just drop it."

"I'll drop it if you agree to two things. First, you'll forget about leaving the ranch, and secondly, you'll tell me if anything happens."

"Anything," of course, was a polite way of saying *pregnant*. Either politeness or he couldn't bring himself to say the word, Cleo thought spitefully.

"Your conditions are acceptable if you agree to staying away from me," she said icily.

"I already told you I would."

It wasn't a matter of belief for Cleo. It was just that her choices were so limited.

"Fine," she said stiffly. "We understand each other."

"Yeah, right," Chance muttered under his breath.

"What was that?"

"I said all right. We understand each other."

Six

In the ensuing days Cleo had a hard time with the intensity and persistence of memory. Spotting Chance across the compound brought an aching catch to her throat; working with him at close range created an almost unbearable emotional turmoil.

She hid it all, and told herself this time of agony would pass. Guilt plagued her almost constantly, and dread. Anxiously she prayed for a normal cycle and awaited her monthly visitor.

But there weren't so many episodes with men in her life that she could belittle or minimize the emotional impact of what had taken place with Chance. To be honest, her affair with Jake had been child's play compared to those few minutes with Chance, maybe because she was older now. Or maybe because of her years-long avoidance of men on any level. What stunned her again and again, every time she thought of it, was her shocking participation, her complete separation from reality. In Chance's arms she had lost touch with everything she valued, and she had never once, before that fateful day, suspected her own capacity for such reckless behavior.

It was a bitter pill to swallow. Not that it would happen again, though she wasn't hanging her hat on Chance's promise to stay away from her. In this case, she had to rely entirely on her own good sense.

Working in the barn one morning, she glanced through a window to see Chance coming out of the house. She stared, then squinted her eyes to see him better. He was wearing a suit and tie, and even with distance blurring details, Cleo recognized the excellent quality of his clothing.

Her heart began beating in double time. He was gorgeous, dressed up as she'd never seen him, and for what? Chance strode to the Blazer, and Cleo saw that the vehicle had not only been washed but bore the shiny gloss of a hand-rubbed polish job, which he must have administered himself.

She moved to the open door of the barn and watched the Blazer driving off. The void in her stomach grew larger as the vehicle got smaller, and when it was out of range she left the barn and, without stopping to consider what she was doing, hurried across the compound to the house.

Slowing her pace, she walked into the house and then the kitchen with a nonchalant expression. "Hi, Joe."

"Cleo," Joe grunted in his usual grumpy way.

"I was looking for Chance."

"He's gone."

"Yes, I saw him driving away. Will he be gone long?"

"Don't know. He didn't say."

"He . . . seemed to be dressed differently."

"Yep. All decked out in a suit," Joe confirmed.

"And he didn't mention where he was going?" Cleo asked casually.

Joe cocked a curious eyebrow at her. "All he said was 'See ya later,' when he left."

The emptiness in Cleo got bigger, but questioning Joe was doing nothing but arousing his curiosity. "Well...it wasn't anything that can't wait," she said in a tone that implied a true necessity to talk to Chance and resignation at the delay.

Leaving the house, the last few minutes suddenly registered. Cleo's stomach knotted and she stopped and actually reeled for a moment. Was she demented? Why should it matter to her where Chance went or what he was doing? She didn't care what he did, dammit! Checking up on him was insane.

The truth struck without mercy. She was jealous! But jealous of what? Did she think he'd gone off to be with another woman?

"Oh, God," Cleo whispered, covering her face with her hands. He had every right to do anything he pleased. The tearing in her stomach hurt, a feeling she'd never before experienced. She wasn't herself where Chance was concerned. This had to stop.

Dropping her hands and drawing a determined breath, Cleo walked to her house and went in. "Rosie, I'm going for a long ride. Would you like to come along?"

The little girl grinned happily. "I finished the breakfast dishes, Mama."

"Thanks, sweetheart. Do you want to come with me?"

"Yes. I'll go get my boots."

Chance got back around four that afternoon. He went directly to the study, draped his suit coat and tie over a chair and sat at the desk. A feeling of exhilaration kept a faint smile on his lips; the day had been productive and satisfying. With a pen, yellow pad and the desk calculator, he put some numbers together, rearranging or changing them to fit the ideas darting around in his mind.

Yesterday's phone call from John Holby had surprised Chance, as had the banker's invitation to have lunch with him today. But their conversation had taken Chance's imagination to new heights.

"I took the liberty of making a few discreet inquiries about you, Chance. Hope you don't mind."

"Not at all, John."

"Your family is well thought of in financial circles."

"My grandfather's doing, John."

"Perhaps, but the Saxon name carries a lot of weight. In any case, I wondered if you would be interested in a business suggestion."

"I'm very interested," Chance replied.

John had explained a line of credit with his bank, a type of loan unfamiliar to Chance. *"It would be collateralized by the ranch, of course, but it's money that would be available only if you need it. In other words, you wouldn't be borrowing a specific sum and letting it lie in your bank account while paying interest on money you weren't using. Do you follow me?"*

Chance had grasped the concept at once, and after lunch had accompanied John back to the bank to start the paperwork necessary for a line of credit for the Kidd River Ranch. It was a sound and sensible approach to a loan. If and when he needed cash, he could draw the precise sum against his credit line merely by using one of the special checks provided by the bank. It was not a plan to use without caution, certainly never for fanciful notions. But it would level out the highs and lows of the cattle business, and preclude depleting his herd prematurely for operating cash.

Chance was discovering the excitement of the business world, and beginning to grasp how one could not only stay afloat but make money by shrewdly shifting assets and liabilities. The risks, oddly enough, were as stimulating as the hope of success, and for the first time, Chance had a glimpse of the strong forces that had motivated his grandfather into making a fortune.

When Joe announced supper was ready, Chance went to the dining room to eat. He talked with Pete about the cattle and ranch—always the main topics at the dinner table—but he thought about Cleo. He wanted to see her, and not in her capacity of foreman, either. He'd been picking his words again, walking on eggs around her, lying through his teeth in an effort to convey disinterest.

He was interested, all right. He didn't only want to see Cleo, he *wanted* Cleo. Exactly as she'd been that day in her van, uninhibited, eager, passionate. He'd been waking up during the night in a cold sweat from wanting her, and if that wasn't being interested in a woman, nothing was.

The thing was, Cleo's threats to leave should Chance's attentions persist were losing impetus for him. In the first place, no employee was indispensable. In the second, his confidence with the ranch was gaining ground daily. Not that he was so smug to think he didn't have a lot to learn yet. But if Cleo walked away tomorrow, the ranch would survive. It was himself he wondered about.

He wanted to ask her out, to take her dancing, maybe, or to a good restaurant. Lord knew he didn't have money to throw away on expensive restaurants, but the thought of sitting across a candle-lit table from Cleo was too energizing to crassly weigh it against mere money.

He thanked Joe for a good meal and followed Pete outside. The cowpuncher lit a cigarette and began ambling toward the bunkhouse. Chance stood there and looked at Cleo's house, which he realized he'd never set foot in.

They were living a lie, he thought grimly. Pretending every day that nothing had happened between them, and worse, that it wasn't going to happen again.

Tisk and Task came along, and Chance bent over to scratch the two dogs' ears. "How ya doing, fellas?" They were a pair of motley mutts, but they'd become a part of the ranch to Chance, and Rosie loved them.

A sprinkling of rain brought Chance's eyes up to scan the dark clouds, which had moved in very quickly. The atmosphere was suddenly heavy, the day's final light fading fast.

Instead of returning to the house, Chance sprinted to the barn. He stood in the frame of the barn door, leaning against one side with his hands in his pants pockets, watching the raindrops plopping in the dust of the compound. The air freshened and cooled as moisture dampened the earth.

The rain fell harder, pelting the ground. The deluge felt good to Chance. Darkness was coming fast, cloaking the buildings, blurring the scene, but he found pleasure in surveying the watery shadows and making plans for the future of the ranch.

He heard someone running before he saw who it was. Stepping back from the door, Chance waited for Cleo to dash in. She had a jacket tented over her head and immediately went for the massive door.

"I'll close it," he announced.

She jumped. "What on earth...? I didn't see you!"

"I was watching the rain."

Cleo arranged the jacket around her shoulders to camouflage the thin cotton robe she'd put on after her bath. She'd gotten out of the tub and dawdled in the bathroom, and not until the water had vanished down the drain had she heard how hard it was raining.

"I always close the barn door in this kind of downpour," she explained. "But if you're going to do it..."

"Wait," Chance said quietly. "Stay a minute."

She took in his dark pants and white shirt, and remembered her battle with jealousy this morning. The pain of those moments renewed itself, and she sighed unhappily and turned to the rainy scene, hugging the jacket around herself.

Chance's voice came from behind her, low and rife with tension. "It's not working, is it?"

She hesitated, but didn't pretend not to know what he meant. "Not...very well."

"What are you afraid of with me?"

"A lot of things."

"Tell me."

"Chance...I can't. What good would it do anyway? You're who you are and I'm...different."

"I like your differences, Cleo."

"For the time being."

"Do you want a commitment?"

She shivered. "I don't know what I want. I liked my life before you came here. I was...content."

"Self-insulation isn't contentment, Cleo."

She glanced back at his shadowy form. "Call it what you want, but my life was going smoothly. So was Rosie's."

"I haven't disrupted Rosie's life. Speak for yourself."

"If my life is disrupted, so is Rosie's," Cleo said stubbornly. "Leaving here would bother her a great deal."

"It would bother you a hell of a lot more. Admit it, Cleo."

Her shoulders lifted in a resigned heave. "All right, I admit it. This has been home for five years. It means...it represents security." She shook her head, almost sadly. "It's not the same now."

"Because I'm here."

"Not just because you're here, but because..." Cleo took another direction. "I was glad when you came. I didn't know what to do about the lack of money. I couldn't figure out why no one cared about the place."

"I care about it."

"Do you?" Cleo turned around. "Aren't you getting just a little bit bored with the never-ending responsibility?" *Isn't that why you dressed up and spent the day somewhere else?*

Chance studied her pale face in the gathering darkness. "I've never been less bored in my life." He took a forward step, on the verge of telling her about today, about the meeting with Holby and what he had discovered about himself.

But she removed the jacket from her shoulders and began to lift it to her head. "I've got to get back. I told Rosie I'd only be gone a few minutes. Don't forget to close..."

Chance reacted without intent. His right arm snaked out and curled around her waist, hauling her up against him. His mouth crashed down on hers, startling both of them, and it felt so right, so damned right, that he kept on kissing her, hard.

When it sank in that she wasn't fighting him and was, in fact, kissing him back, his lips gentled. "Cleo...sweetheart..." His mouth moved over her face, tasting the remnants of raindrops on her skin. He shoved the jacket aside and stroked her back, whispering, "What are you wearing?"

"An old robe. Chance... don't do this." Her own voice was so breathless and husky, Cleo barely recognized it. Besides, telling him not to do something that she could easily stop by taking one step away from him was slightly ludicrous.

His response to the feeble request was to kiss her again, to take her lips in a slow, languorous mating, to tease the tip of her tongue with his and to slide his hands down her back to her bottom.

All of Cleo's good intentions were disappearing. The female in her couldn't get close enough to Chance. His shirt was damp and smelled of soap, the outdoors and him. His warmth drew her as a magnet did iron filings. Her hands slid up his chest to his throat, and then to the back of his neck, where her fingers threaded into the hair above his collar.

"You can be so sweet," Chance murmured.

She tilted her head back to see his face. "And so easy?"

"No, not easy. No one could ever accuse you of that, Cleo." His lips sought hers again.

She indulged the desire racking her body and let him kiss her, thinking dimly that she could happily live out her life in his arms. Her breasts ached from the contact with his chest, while the union of their lower bodies practically destroyed her nervous system. His arms around her were utterly masculine, muscular, possessive, thrilling, as were the long thighs heating hers through two layers of clothing.

Except her layer was all but nonexistent. Not expecting to run into anyone in the rain, she hadn't given the flimsy old robe a thought. It was years old, nearly threadbare from the washer and dryer, and provided very little protection, especially since she wore nothing under it.

Her state of undress was an unmerciful torment for Chance. The thin fabric was as seductive as silk, and slid between his hands and Cleo's skin. His mouth opened on hers, enveloping hers, then moved to take her lower lip between his teeth while he began working up the skirt of her robe.

Cleo could hear the pounding of her own heart, and feel the thudding of Chance's. The rain had an alluring rhythm and created a musky, murky atmosphere within the barn. Chance wasn't moving fast, but his ardor was as obvious as the downpour, as was her own. She realized exactly where this was heading when his hand glided upward beneath her robe.

"Wait," she stammered raggedly, and moved to hold his hand still through the robe.

"Cleo, come to the house with me," Chance pleaded.

"No! Joe..." Cleo backed away, taking refuge in distance.

"If he hasn't left yet, he soon will. Come later, when you're sure. The door is never locked. Just come in and..." His voice trailed off at the expression on her face. "There's nothing wrong with you and I being together. I can't come to your house because of Rosie, but you can come to mine."

"I told you I wouldn't do that." She couldn't look at him. His good looks dazzled her, and she was afraid of succumbing. Her blood was urging her to do so, her heart, her pulse, the female core of her.

But the one time of her life she'd given everything had concluded in heartbreak, and she didn't trust Chance. Comparing him to Jake was all wrong. The only thing the two of them had in common was coloring. Jake had been as deceitful as any man could be with a woman, and Chance wasn't deceitful. But neither was he her kind of person. The evidence of his background struck her every day, his speech, his mannerisms, his clothing. She was an interlude for him, the only woman on the ranch, and possibly provocative because she was different than the women he'd known before.

Besides, they had already taken one monumental risk and she still didn't know its outcome.

Frustration gripped Chance. Sexual frustration, to be sure, but more than that, the frustration of not getting through to Cleo on any level.

"You don't trust me," he said, hoping she would deny the charge. She didn't. "Cleo, for God's sake, what have I done to make you so distrustful?"

"You don't understand."

"How could I? Explain it to me. *Make* me understand."

Cleo's gaze went to the open door. It was pouring rain, but she would have to brave getting drenched to put an end to this unsettling session.

The episode was more than "unsettling" for Chance. He'd never begged a woman before, never had to, and his pussyfooting with Cleo was beginning to turn his stomach. He'd done a lot of changing since his arrival at the ranch and considered the changes improvements. He was stronger, both physically and emotionally, harder than he'd been, but the most lenient judge couldn't label his behavior with Cleo as strong.

Bending over, he scooped her jacket from the floor, then held it out to her. "I've played it all wrong with you, Cleo."

With wider eyes, she took the jacket. "What's that supposed to mean?"

"It means that it's over," Chance stated flatly. "If there's ever another pass between us, it'll come from you."

His disdain rocketed through Cleo, shocking her to anger. "Don't hold your breath!"

"Oh, I won't, believe me. I thought we had something special, Cleo. Apparently I was dead wrong. You've lived one way for so long, you can't see anything else. Well, that's just fine. You won't be bothered again, not by me."

His hard line stunned Cleo. She could walk away from the ranch right now and he wouldn't try to stop her! The realization sent a ripple of nausea through her system. Everything had changed so fast. Before her very eyes, Chance had become a different man, a tougher, don't-give-a-damn-what-she-did man. It was so unexpected, she couldn't think of a comeback.

Furious and embarrassed that tears would dare to form at this debasing moment, Cleo turned her back and slid her arms into the jacket. "I've got to go."

"No one's stopping you," Chance pointed out coldly. "Run, Cleo. Run away. Don't let anyone get through that righteous coat of armor you wear. I've got the picture now. One man hurt you so you wrote us all off. You don't know how to trust, Cleo, and that makes you a dangerous woman."

Her, dangerous? The idea was so preposterous, Cleo gasped. She whirled. "Stop with the melodrama, Chance. You're only mad because I said no. Your ego can't take it. You're nothing but a spoiled-rotten brat who had everything his way for so long he can't adjust to the real world."

"I'm adjusting real fast," Chance retorted. "You're half-right, Cleo. I did have everything my way for a long time. But you know something, honey? I *like* the real world, I like the man I'm becoming and the fact that no one's out there with a fat bankroll to pay the bills. Anything I do here will be *my* accomplishment. Any friends I make will be *my* friends and not hangers-on because my name is Saxon. I'm here to stay, Cleo, and if you can't live with that, then I guess you'll have to do something else."

His attitude nearly floored Cleo. Her first furious impulse was to get the hell away from the Kidd River Ranch and never look back.

But in the next breath she realized he was only paraphrasing her own words. She'd said virtually the same thing to him more than once: If we can't work together in impersonal harmony, it's best that I leave.

She squared her shoulders. "I respect you more for what you just said than for anything else I've heard from you. Let's clear the air once and for all. Do you want me to continue as your foreman?"

It was Chance's turn to look stunned, though he managed a reasonably normal "Yes."

"Well, I'd like to stay."

They stared at each other, heads up, chins set, both recognizing the honesty of the moment. Maybe their first, Chance thought. He'd like to take this remarkable honesty further, he realized, into their personal relationship. Would the day come when Cleo could speak as freely about that as she did about her job?

"Then stay," he said rather brusquely.

"Thanks, I will." Cleo moved to the door again, grateful to whatever force had stopped her tears before she'd made a fool of herself. Bringing the jacket up to her head, she glanced back at Chance. "I apologize for calling you a spoiled brat."

Then she was gone. Chance stepped to the door and watched her running through the rain. Cleo was under his skin, *way* under. He wouldn't get over wanting her just because he'd made that little speech, but he wouldn't make another pass if his life depended on it.

Walking out into the rain, he closed the barn door and then started for the house, slowly. Maybe the rain would take the place of a cold shower, he thought with some cynicism. It was certain he needed something to cool him off.

Seven

Their truce felt like something tangible. It lay between Cleo and Chance while they rode together, discussed or did chores together, or when one of them merely spotted the other at a distance. His position as employer and hers as employee seemed more pronounced these days, deliberately, as though that invisible line would serve as a barrier to further intimacy.

The hay was cut and stored, a job that took up most of a week. The local blacksmith spent two days on the ranch checking the horses' hooves and putting on new shoes when necessary. The cows were separated from the steers, and the females were driven to lower ground in preparation of the insemination process.

Although almost constantly busy, Cleo lived with an unfamiliar restlessness. An edginess. Life on the Kidd River Ranch wasn't the same as before Chance's arrival and she couldn't pretend it was. Not to herself, at any rate, though she did a fair job of it with the others.

One day Rosie asked, "Mama, when are we going camping?"

Cleo had been promising a camping trip, and Rosie's question prompted a decision. It would be good to get away from the pressure for a few days. "How about this weekend, honey? I'll talk to Chance about taking some time off."

That evening she walked into the silence of the big house and called, "Chance?"

"I'm in the study."

Cleo had been spending odd hours in the study keeping up the book work. There was only the one desk, so often when she sat down to write checks or make entries into the ledgers, there was evidence of Chance's usage remaining on the desk. At first she had scanned the yellow pads with their pages of notations and numbers, but none of it had made any sense and she'd begun to merely set the pads aside.

He had one in front of him tonight, she noticed as she walked into the study. There was a glass at his elbow containing a pale amber liquid and ice cubes, and a pen in his hand. He got to his feet. "Do you need to use the study?"

"No, not at all. I'd like to talk to you for a minute, but I don't want to interrupt."

"No problem." Chance gestured to a chair. "Sit down." His gaze flicked over Cleo's white jeans and red-and-white striped T-shirt. Her skin was darker than when he'd first met her, tanned from working outdoors under the summer sun. As usual when she wasn't wearing a hat, her honey-gold hair was smooth from her face and tied back.

As she walked into the room and to the chair near the desk, Chance's attention lingered—furtively—on her flat stomach and the arousing pitch of her hipbones. Jeans were perfect for a woman of Cleo's lean build, he thought, and those snowy-white pants were particularly appealing.

He cleared his throat and sat down. It was ironic that the better Cleo looked in clothes, the more he wanted to get her out of them.

"I'd like to take a few days off," Cleo stated, getting right to the point. Except for discussions regarding some aspect of the ranch, she and Chance didn't converse easily anymore.

Chance nodded. "You're the judge of your own time, Cleo. You don't need my permission."

"I disagree."

His sigh was inward and private. "In that case, you have it."

"Thank you. Rosie and I are going camping. I'll leave on Friday morning and return on Monday."

The word *camping* brought a flood of memories to Chance, every one of them connected to Cleo's van. The instant ache in his groin wasn't deserved, he thought wryly. Why in hell couldn't he put that aspect of their relationship in the past and forget it? "Uh . . . great. I'm sure Rosie's excited about the weekend. Where will you go?"

"Probably to Clear Lake. It's not far and has good camping facilities." Cleo stood up. "Well, that's all I needed to see you about. Sorry for the interruption." She glanced curiously at the yellow pad on the desk, wondering what all those numbers represented.

Chance registered the direction of her gaze. "I'm figuring on increasing the herd next season. This ranch will support three times the number of cattle we have now."

Cleo's eyes widened. "The land will support a much larger herd, yes, but how . . . ?" She stopped. Finances were Chance's business, not hers.

"A bank loan," Chance volunteered.

The thought of unnecessary debt gave Cleo a chill. "With the land as collateral?"

"You don't approve."

"It's not my place to pass such opinions."

Chance's eyes narrowed. "I'm asking you straight out. Do you approve of a larger herd?"

"A larger herd, yes."

"There's only one way to expand, Cleo."

"There's only one way to expand *quickly*," she amended. "Your land is free and clear, which is the very goal a good many ranchers strive to reach throughout years of struggle."

"I'm sure that's true. I realize there's risk involved, but profit is crucial, Cleo. I've worked it out on paper a dozen different ways, and the conclusion is always the same. Even taking the interest on bank loans into account, there are good profits to be made from buying and selling cattle at the right time of year. The larger the herd, the larger the profit."

Cleo sank back to her chair. "Have you considered market fluctuations? There are no guarantees that you'll receive the same good price for beef next year that you can sell for this year."

"If there's one thing I've learned lately, it's that there are no guarantees for anything in life."

She couldn't debate that point, but she still didn't like the idea of a mortgage hanging over the ranch.

"Cleo, a successful year in any business depends on how many times one can turn the same dollar," Chance said quietly. "That's what I'm thinking about, borrowing what I need in the spring to buy young steers, selling them in the fall and repaying the loan. Eventually the ranch will operate on its own capital and loans won't be necessary."

"And the cows?"

Chance took a second before answering as his plans for the future of the Kidd River Ranch were different than its history, and he suspected Cleo would balk. "I'm getting out of the breeding business. It costs money to feed the cows during a harsh winter and they need more attention than steers, specifically the births, the castration of the male calves in the spring and the cows' insemination in August, all of which requires additional manpower. Without the cows those steps will be eliminated and we can continue to operate with one man, Pete, for most of the year."

"Well," Cleo said after a rather stunned moment. "Looks like you've been busy."

Chance's eyes held hers. "I hope you approve."

And if I don't? He'd grasped the cattle business so quickly and seemed so positive about future plans. Changes weren't easy for Cleo. For five years she'd adhered to routine—each season had its own. She had done some of what Chance was talking about, buying and selling steers, but the new calves each spring had always given her the most satisfaction.

"It will relieve some of your work, as well," Chance pointed out. "You won't have to keep track of breeding records."

"That hasn't been a problem," she said with some coolness.

Her attitude was obvious. "I'm sorry you don't approve. I'd really hoped you would."

She wanted to point out that his decision could be hasty and premature for a man who was still a greenhorn, but she was an employee, not a partner, and she stifled the impulse. Rising again, she took a breath. "Well, I hope it turns out as you... uh, hope it will."

Chance stood up. "That's the key word, Cleo, hope. As I said, it comes out just fine on paper."

"You'll be selling the cows then?"

Chance cleared his throat. "They're already sold. Maybe you know the buyer, Jim Candleberry."

The Candleberry ranch was well-known in the area. "I know who he is. He wants the cows before insemination?"

"He's going to breed them with his own bulls. He'll be picking them up the first of next week."

Losing the cows was a shock. August suddenly loomed as an idle month, when ordinarily it was one of the most demanding of the year. Chance had every right to make a decision with such far-reaching consequences, but it stung Cleo that he hadn't even attempted to discuss it with her beforehand.

But then, she realized, they hadn't been exactly chatty with each other lately. This was their lengthiest conversation since that rainy evening in the barn. It seemed like a propitious opportunity for passing on another piece of information.

"Just so you know," she said tonelessly, "there's no longer any possibility of..." The word stuck in her throat.

Chance was watching her closely, and her face suddenly
flamed. She had wanted to present the facts unemotionally,
but the entire subject was rooted in emotion and difficult to
introduce.

"There's no possibility of what, Cleo?" Chance asked
softly, though he knew precisely which word had caused her
red face.

"I'm...not pregnant." She blurted out the words, then
added, "I'm sure you're enormously relieved."

"Are you?"

"Relieved? Well, yes, of course!" She couldn't read the
strange expression in his eyes, but discomfited by it, she began backing toward the door. "I'll let you get back to...your
numbers."

They were growing farther apart by the day, Chance realized with a thinning of his lips. Working together wasn't
influencing Cleo's attitude in the least. He'd sworn to avoid
the personal aspect of their relationship, but he sensed feelings from her that had nothing to do with the ranch and it
was becoming increasingly apparent that she would never
make any sort of move to express them.

"Cleo!"

She was nearly through the door. "Yes?"

Chance rounded the desk and walked over to her. His
hands itched to touch her, to draw her into his arms. The
house was empty, almost mocking in its silence, and if privacy had been the only missing ingredient in their relationship, they had it now.

"Stay and talk," he said, keeping the urgency storming
his system out of his voice. "About the ranch, my plans. I'd
like your input."

"You're wrong. You wouldn't like it," she rebutted flatly.

"You see nothing positive in my decision?"

"My approval would add nothing to your success."

"Your approval is important to me." Unbidden, his gaze
slid from her face to her throat, then farther down, to the
swells of her breasts within the soft knit of her shirt. Desire
was streaking through him, affecting his voice, increasing

his daring. "You're important to me." His eyes slowly lifted to search hers for a response.

Their wild lovemaking in the van lay on the path of their gazes. They knew each other's body, they had experienced passion together, and those incredible minutes were suddenly in the very air they were breathing.

But they had also vowed, each of them, that it wouldn't happen again. Chance had told her, point-blank, that another pass between them would never come from him. Looking at her now, he cursed his resentful words in the barn. That's all it had been, resentment because she kept denying the powerful attraction between them. He could see it in her eyes right now, the glaze of memory and the potency of her own desire.

He inched closer, not touching her, but crowding her back against the wall. She raised a hand to stop his advance, and it landed on his chest. He lifted his own hand and covered hers, and they stood there and suffered the torment of denial.

Chance licked his lips. His eyes, Cleo saw, were smoky and hot. Her own heartbeat was choking her. She hadn't come to the study for another test of her willpower, but it was almost impossible to remember why she had come.

"I want you," he whispered. "I've never wanted any woman more. You're in my dreams at night and controlling my thoughts and moods during the day. My showers are cold and miserable because of you. This isn't a pass. I told you I wouldn't do that again and I won't. But you're driving me crazy, Cleo, and I have to ask myself why. Maybe you know the answer."

The word *love* flashed into her mind, but she pushed it away. If he started talking about love, she wouldn't believe him, and she didn't want to hear any lies.

"I have no answer," she said, low and tensely. "Please move back so I can leave." Though the door was within reach, she was hemmed in by a large bookcase on her right and the wall at her back. Laying her hand on his chest had been a mistake. He was clasping it to his shirt, and the heat of his body was radiating up her arm through her palm.

Life had been so simple before Chance Saxon's intrusion, she thought on a stifled groan. Nothing had stirred her emotions beyond the fervent love she held for Rosie, and she'd been happy, dammit, happy! If Chance was miserable taking cold showers, good! He deserved misery from some direction after what he'd been causing her.

But it was her own response to his nearness that held her transfixed and frightened. Whatever she said to him, whatever he said to her, nothing stopped the volatile desire they both lived with. It was omnipotent, apparently, indestructible, awaiting each and every tiny opportunity to erupt and engulf them. One word, one sign from her and Chance would sweep her into his arms. The image was tantalizing, making her skin tingle, her breath come in short gasps.

His hand moved on hers. There was a plea in his eyes. *Do it, Cleo. Let me know it's okay to proceed. I want you.*

Cleo wanted him, too. Every cell in her body seemed to be yearning for him, straining toward him. With a low moan, she closed her eyes and let her head fall forward so that her forehead was against his shirt.

Chance sucked in air and put his arms around her. She came closer, and her body against his released restraint. He began kissing her, taking her mouth, moving his lips over her face. "Cleo..." His voice was raspy, unnatural. She brought him higher, quicker than any woman ever had. Control with Cleo was a laughable concept. He had no control with her and didn't care. She was beautiful, exciting, and he was wild for her.

He kicked the study door closed, just on the off chance that someone should wander into the house. Hearing the slam, Cleo shuddered. It was going to happen here, and there was nothing she could do to stop it, nothing she wanted to do.

They began struggling with clothing. Chance lifted her knit top over her head, taking her ribbon with it. Freed, her hair fell around her face. He dug his hands into the silky strands, and held her head and kissed her lips. His tongue probed the moist depths of her mouth, and she moaned and blindly groped for the buttons on his shirt. Lifting one foot from the floor, she twined her leg around his, and rubbed her pelvis against the hard, protruding mass behind his fly.

They had to separate to remove jeans and boots, but it was a hurried few moments. Naked, they came together and lost themselves in hot, openmouthed kisses.

Cleo could barely speak. "Do you have a condom?"

"Yes...yes." Impatient, he crouched at his jeans and dug into his wallet. In seconds he was with her again, kissing her, lifting her off the floor. Her legs wound around his hips. He placed her back to the wall and slid into her heat with a ragged groan.

Cleo tried to bury her face in his neck, but he growled, "Look at me," and his eyes, hot and smoldering, held hers while he loved her. She could feel a trembling in the muscles of his arms and legs, hear his rasping breaths. Her thoughts, though, were focused on the pleasure within herself, the building of tension, the bliss that kept getting closer and closer. It crept up on her, each powerful thrust of his body bringing it nearer.

Her moans became whispered endearments, breathless and from deep in her throat. "Chance...Chance..."

His passion swelled and demanded. He lifted her higher, went deeper, faster. "Cleo...baby..."

They met the stars together, clutching each other, crying out together. For a second they were still, unmoving, then Chance gave in to the draining weakness in his legs and sank to the floor, bringing Cleo with him.

Her face was burrowed in his throat. Her arms around him were trembling, her skin was damp and sweaty. With his chin he nudged her forehead, urging her head up. He saw tears on her cheeks and her eyes wouldn't quite meet his.

She said three hoarse words, "You won...again."

"It's not a contest. Look at me."

Her tear-filled eyes rose to his. "I can't fight you. Why do I even try?"

"There's no reason to fight me. Cleo, we can't be in the same room without wanting each other. I can't ride a horse next to yours without thinking about undressing you. I get hard if I see you from a quarter-mile away. I've never been so obsessed with a woman. My own imagination is tearing me apart."

She sighed, wearily, because she was doing the same sort of foolish things with him. She'd been trying her level best to ignore and elude his magnetism, but behind every other thought was him, his body, his hands, his mouth.

The camping trip wasn't only a good idea, it was necessary to her mental health. She needed to get off by herself and do some heavy-duty thinking, and though Rosie would be with her, there would be ample opportunities to do so.

"Don't look so stricken," Chance said softly. They were still joined, and with any encouragement at all from her, he would repeat their lovemaking. Not in the same hot, greedy way, but slowly, deliciously. A new heat reflected in his eyes. "I want you in a bed. I want to wake up in the night and feel you next to me."

"A sexual fantasy," Cleo whispered. Her voice became stronger. "Rosie's alone. I have to go home." When Chance merely kept staring at her, she added, "She could come looking for me." It wasn't true. Rosie never came to the big house without explicit permission, but Chance didn't need to know that. She was worried, Cleo realized, that he might try to persuade her again, and who knew better than she how potent was his brand of persuasion?

But Rosie's name stalled Chance's returning desire. The one thing he would never do was try to corrupt Cleo's concern for her daughter. He admired the indisputable love between them, and knew his high regard had roots in his own motherless childhood.

"Yes," he said quietly. "You have to go." He pressed his lips to hers, gently because he felt enormous tenderness for Cleo at this moment. His head lifted to see her face, and the startled expression in her eyes warmed him. Obviously she didn't expect tenderness from him. He smiled. "Can you finally believe I care for you?"

She believed he wanted her—how could she not—and that he would never let her be as long as she was on the ranch. But believing anything beyond the no-longer deniable sexuality between them was taking a step into alien territory for Cleo.

Instead of replying, she disentangled herself from his lap and reached for her underwear. She turned her back to put on her bra.

"Cleo? Aren't you going to answer my question?"

Rising, Cleo scrambled into her panties and then began shoving her feet into the legs of her jeans. She turned around to see him zipping the fly of his own jeans. "I believe you want me," she said evenly. "Like this."

"And that's it?"

"What do you want me to say, Chance?"

"What you're thinking."

Cleo worked her knit top down over her head and adjusted it in place. "Fine," she said sharply. "I'm thinking that I'm putty in your hands, that all you have to do is touch me and I behave like some mindless sl..."

"Don't say it!" Chance bellowed, cutting the demeaning word in midsyllable. "Dammit, don't you think you do the same thing to me?"

Cleo smoothed back her hair and began looking around the floor for her ribbon. "Men can sleep around and not be labeled anything but cool and sexy. A stud," she said bitterly. "You know what easy women are called the same as I do."

"You're not easy!"

"So you've said." She arched a cynical eyebrow. "What do you call it? What's your name for a woman who does an immediate meltdown every time you put your hands on her?"

"I've got plenty of labels for you, Cleo, and not one of them is an insult. How about beautiful? Sensual? Intelligent?"

"Yeah, I'm intelligent, all right," she muttered sarcastically. Spotting the ribbon near the base of the bookcase, Cleo bent over for it. She tied her hair back with jerky movements. "What you and I are involved in is an affair, Chance. Don't try to gloss it over with pretty words."

"The women I knew before you liked pretty words."

She sent him a scathing glare. "I'd just as soon not hear about your other conquests, if you don't mind." His near nudity registered. His bare chest with its sexy patch of black hair made her stomach ache. The way his unbuttoned jeans hung on his lean hips made her grit her teeth. Why in hell didn't he get dressed?

The word "conquests" brought a faint chuckle to Chance's lips. There'd been other women, sure, but he'd never considered himself as a conqueror of female virtue.

Cleo didn't find his amusement at all to her liking. "If you see something funny in this situation, by all means share it."

"It's not a situation, for God's sake," Chance said with some disgust. "Let's not overdramatize, Cleo. We're an ordinary man and woman who find each other extremely potent. You knock my socks off, honey, and I don't think it's conceited for me to say I do the same to you."

"You're not at all ordinary, so stop kidding yourself," Cleo retorted. "There's not another rancher in the county with your background, maybe not in the whole damned state. Or if there is, I haven't run into him."

Chance regarded her through narrow eyes. "You can't get beyond who I was before I came here, can you? The fact that my family was wealthy? Well, let me tell you something, Cleo. I never contributed one dime or one minute's time to that wealth. Nor did my brothers. Every dollar in the family coffers was put there by our grandfather, and I'm not one bit proud of how I lived before coming here. So you see, your scorn for my past is no deeper than my own.

"But I'm more optimistic than you are, Cleo. I've stopped dwelling on old mistakes and live in the present, hopeful of the future. Maybe it's something you should try, because it's pretty damned obvious you're having a hard time letting go of your own past."

She had gradually stiffened throughout his little speech, but the worst blow was his painfully accurate summation of her attitude. She *was* living in the past, carrying enormous guilt for falling in love with the wrong man, a married man. Her not knowing about Jake's marital ties hadn't mattered in the guilt game; she *should* have known.

Dazed by her sudden confusion, Cleo's fingertips rose to her throbbing temples. After Jake, she had denied every other male-female liaison because of self-reproach, *not* because of good sense, as she'd believed. Chance was the first man who'd broken through her defenses, which undoubtedly meant something, but what? That she was sex-starved? That she'd finally reached the point where her defenses were no longer effective?

"Cleo?" There was concern in Chance's voice, because she looked so shaken. "Hey, I didn't mean to upset you." He moved to her and tried to take her hands, which she avoided by flailing her arms. She stumbled to the door. "Cleo!"

Ignoring him completely, Cleo ran through the house.

Scowling, Chance stepped through the study door. "Dammit, Cleo," he shouted. "Will you never stop running away?"

Eight

For Rosie's sake, Cleo maintained a smiling face while she drove to Clear Lake. They sang songs together, and played games. Counting out-of-state license plates was one of Rosie's favorites, as was Twenty Questions.

The van was loaded down with food, blankets, clothing and fishing rods. Cleo had tucked in a few books, some for Rosie, some for herself. Their bathing suits were important cargo, as Rosie was excited about going swimming.

"We'll camp right by the lake, won't we, Mama?"

"If we can, honey. Sometimes the lake spots are already taken."

"I sure hope we can. I want to run from the van in the morning and jump right into the lake."

Cleo laughed. "Well, even if you have to run a little farther, I'm sure that can be arranged."

"Did you ask Chance to go with us?"

Cleo's startled eyes darted from the highway to her daughter. "No, I didn't. Why? Would you like him going with us?"

Rosie sighed. "Well...he doesn't have anyone to go camping with like we do. I bet he wishes he did. I bet he gets lonesome sometimes."

"Pete doesn't have anyone to camp with, either, Rosie. Neither does Joe."

"They could go camping together, couldn't they?"

It wasn't Pete or Joe who had Rosie concerned, Cleo realized. It was Chance. The man had not only mesmerized the mother, but he'd also worked his magic on the daughter!

"Let's sing another song," Cleo suggested. "How about 'Row, Row, Row Your Boat'?"

Rosie giggled. "You start first, Mama."

They pulled into the Clear Lake Campground around noon. Rosie piled out of the van to follow her mother into the registration cabin, where an elderly man greeted them with a big smile.

"Hello," Cleo said.

"Natives, I'll bet," the man said.

Cleo smiled. "You're right. Getting many tourists this year?"

"Quite a few. Need a camping space?"

"One by the lake, if possible."

The man grinned down at Rosie. "Could you be the one who wants to stay down by the lake, young lady?"

Rosie smiled shyly. "I'm the one."

The man laughed. "Well, I just happen to have one lakefront space left." He pulled out a registration slip and laid it on the counter in front of Cleo. "Fill this out and the spot is yours."

Rosie was silent until they walked out of the cabin, then she yelled, "Yahoo!" Laughing, Cleo followed her excited daughter to the van, where they climbed in and drove to their appointed space.

It was great, exactly what they'd hoped for; lots of trees, right on the water's edge and far enough away from other campers for privacy. Rosie was all for jumping first into her bathing suit and then the lake.

"After we set up camp, honey," Cleo told her.

"Setting up camp" consisted of several chores, the first of which was attaching the screen and canvas Arizona room to the van, which Cleo had purchased as an optional item when she bought the unit. She had no idea why it was called an "Arizona" room when she purchased it in Montana, but there was no question about the portable room's versatility. It kept out insects, permitted the passage of breezes with its screening, and provided additional and comfortable living space during an outing.

With the canvas room ready for use, Cleo and Rose unfolded their table and chairs within the enclosure. The van's couch was turned into a real bed and made up with sheets and blankets, and Cleo made sure the battery-powered refrigerator was on and working.

She gave Rosie a teasing grin. "Ready to take that swim?"

Rosie let out a gleeful shout and made a dive for her bathing suit. From her eight-year-old point of view, the camping weekend had finally begun.

They fished, played in the pleasantly cool lake water, took hikes, ate goodies and laughed a lot, for two days. By dark each night Cleo was tired enough to sleep very well, but she didn't. Long after Rosie was asleep beside her, Cleo stared into the dark and thought about Chance. About Chance and herself. About herself. About Rosie. The ranch. Life in general. The past. Jake. Her parents, her aunt and uncle, and again, Chance.

It was simple when she finally faced it: She had fallen in love with him. Simple, yes, but heartrending. It was what she had feared from the first, what she had fought so hard against.

Recognizing and acknowledging the truth didn't make Cleo like it. Her relationship with Chance was too close to what she'd had with Jake, based almost entirely on sex, without a future—hopeless.

She had to leave the ranch. Staying would only make matters worse. Chance's promises to leave her be weren't worth the powder it would take to blow them to hell. Maybe he even meant them when he said them, but whenever two seconds of privacy arose between them, he was all over her, and she didn't have the willpower of a flea where he was concerned.

Her break would be clean and final. When she got back on Monday, she would tell Chance she was quitting her job and moving. If he questioned where, she would lie. She could say Billings, or Missoula, or fifty other places, and he'd never know the difference—unless he became interested enough to try to find her later on, which she doubted he'd do. Out of sight, she unhappily figured, out of mind.

On Sunday morning, Cleo and Rosie took another hike. They returned to the campsite at noon. There were other children at the campground, and Rosie stayed outside to play with them while Cleo prepared lunch.

She was in the Arizona room, making sandwiches, when she heard Rosie yelling, "Chance! Chance, you came!" Looking through one of the screened areas in the canvas, Cleo's heart nearly stopped. Walking from the ranch's black Blazer with Rosie's hand in his was Chance. They were talking and laughing like old pals, and her daughter's face was lit up like a Christmas tree.

Cleo's jaw clenched, and when Chance ducked beneath the flap of the Arizona room and came in, she couldn't force herself to say hello.

But Rosie was cordial enough for ten people. "Sit down, Chance. You can use my chair. Mama's making lunch. You can eat with us. Did you bring your bathing suit?"

"Sure did, honey," Chance said softly, speaking to Rosie but looking at Cleo. "Hi."

"Hello," she finally managed to say, albeit distantly.

Rosie looked from her mother to Chance and back to Cleo with a puzzled expression. "Aren't you glad Chance came, Mama?"

Cleo recovered her composure. "Yes, of course. Sit down and eat with us, Chance." She put sandwiches on paper plates and filled glasses with lemonade.

Rosie's perplexity vanished as quickly as it had appeared. "We've been swimming five times," she boasted as she took her plate and glass. "I'll sit on the canvas. You can use my chair, Chance."

"He can use mine, honey. You sit at the table," Cleo said.

"Hey, you two. If anyone gets to sit on the canvas, it's going to be me," Chance said with an exaggerated waggle of his eyebrows that made Rosie giggle. Helping himself to a plate and glass, he plopped down on the canvas floor.

Cleo didn't know where to put herself, though obviously it had to be on her chair at the table. But Chance sitting on the floor made her horribly uncomfortable, and her first bite of sandwich seemed to stick in her throat.

She washed it down with a gulp of lemonade. "So, how did you find us?"

"Wasn't hard. You said Clear Lake, and there's only one on the map." He looked at Rosie. "Been swimming five times, hmm? Is the water warm?"

"It's simply fabulous," Rosie replied in a very grown-up voice, which caused Cleo to nearly choke again.

"Where on earth did you learn that term?" she questioned.

Rosie's on-again, off-again shyness showed. "I don't know."

"There's nothing wrong with it, honey," Cleo explained. "But I've never heard you use it before."

Chance chuckled. "If the water is simply fabulous, I can hardly wait to go swimming. Hey, small fry," he added with a quick glance at Cleo's face. "Want to learn the crawl this afternoon?"

"Yes, yes!" Rosie exclaimed.

"Great. As soon as your mother says it's okay for you to go swimming, I'll give you a lesson."

"Eat your lunch, Rosie," Cleo said quietly. "Then you know the rule."

Rosie sighed and picked up her sandwich. "I have to wait an hour after eating." She turned anxious eyes on Chance. "Will you still be here?"

Chance nodded. "You bet."

During lunch and the ensuing hour, Rosie hovered. She was excited by Chance's appearance and chattered non-stop. Cleo could see in his eyes that he would like to have a few minutes alone with her, but what he wanted didn't prevent him from giving Rosie his full attention.

They walked on the beach, threw pebbles into the water, and talked about fishing and a dozen other topics Rosie introduced. At one point, Cleo heard Chance telling the little girl about fishing in Australia, and she didn't miss how Rosie hung on his every word.

Though Rosie was an unquestionably friendly child, Cleo had never seen her daughter so animated with an adult. The friendship between her boss and her daughter created an ache in Cleo's midsection. She'd seen signs of it before this, but it was so obvious today, so unnerving. Rosie, too, was going to be hurt if she didn't make that break with Chance, and soon, Cleo thought unhappily. The longer she procrastinated, the harder it would be to do.

The swimming lesson was finally underway. Cleo had politely declined an invitation to participate, and she sat on the beach, fully clothed, while Chance in black trunks and Rosie in her two-piece pink suit cavorted in the water. When Rosie actually succeeded in swimming a few overhand strokes, her excitement was infectious, and Cleo applauded enthusiastically.

They swam and practiced and played for hours. Cleo got tired of sitting there and wished she had the nerve to put on her bathing suit and join them. But Chance was showing enough bare skin for both of them, she thought resentfully. All he'd need to develop ideas was for her to parade around half-nude, too.

Around three Cleo brought out cold soft drinks and cookies. "Anyone need a snack?" she called.

Chance came wading out of the water. "Sounds good to me."

Rosie dawdled a little but followed and sprawled in the sand. "Did you see me swimming, Mama?"

"I sure did, honey. You're doing very well." Cleo's eyes met Chance's while she handed him a can of soda. "You're a good teacher. Thank you."

"I enjoyed it, but you're welcome."

Spotting a little girl down the beach, Rosie jumped up. "There's Susie. I want to tell her I can swim now. Is it all right, Mama? May I go tell her?"

"Yes, go ahead," Cleo said.

Chance watched Rosie bounding off. "She's a wonderful kid, Cleo." His gaze moved from Rosie to Cleo. "Probably because you're a wonderful mother."

"Rosie and I understand each other."

"It's more than that, Cleo. You love her and she knows it. Rosie's the most secure child I've ever seen."

"Yes, I love her," Cleo said simply.

"There wouldn't be so many troubled children in the world if their parents treated them the way you treat Rosie."

"Probably not," Cleo agreed. She stopped looking at the lake and looked at him. "There's something I have to tell you."

A discomfiting premonition hit Chance. "What is it?"

"I'm leaving the ranch."

"Cleo," he groaned helplessly. "Dammit, why?"

"Do you really have to ask?" she said with instant anger. "Consider this official notice of my resignation, or whatever one calls quitting a foreman's job. It will take a few days to get packed and arrange for a truck to pick up my furniture, but I should be out of the house and gone no later than the end of next week."

Grimly Chance stared at her. "I hate this. And it's so damned unnecessary."

"That's where you're wrong." Cleo looked at the cookie in her hand and then dropped it back onto the paper plate. "Pete can do anything on the ranch that I can do. You don't need a foreman, anyway, not with only one hired hand. You can use my wages for other things."

"Don't try to bring this down to money, Cleo. You're running scared and we both know it. Uprooting Rosie because of your own insecurities is damned selfish."

Cleo smirked. "I thought you just said I was a good mother."

Sighing, Chance looked away. "You are. I shouldn't have said that." He paused a second. "Where will you go?"

"Uh . . . Denver."

"What's in Denver?"

Why she had named Denver was a complete mystery. But it was a lie, anyway, and didn't matter. "That's what I intend to find out."

"Have you got friends there?"

"Stop with the questions, Chance," she said sharply. "Where I'm going is none of your business."

"You're not even going near Denver, are you? You're planning to disappear and to hell with what I might think." He leaned closer. "Cleo, you can go to the ends of the earth and it won't change what happened between us. You're thinking about it right now, just as I am. You're remembering it all, that day in your van, the other night in the study."

"Of course I remember," Cleo furiously hissed. "It's why I'm leaving. And don't bother to point out again that one mistake shouldn't influence a person's entire life, because you're not in any position to judge, not when you're the second!"

Chance's eyes narrowed. "I'm your second mistake? Are you saying there's been no one since Rosie's father?"

"That's not what I intended to say, but it does happen to be the truth."

Thoughtful, Chance rubbed his jaw. "Why me, then? If you lived without men for eight years, how come me?"

Cleo's heart sank clear to her toes. *Because I was fool enough to fall in love with you!* She tore her eyes from his. "I have no idea."

Chance thought about himself trying to stay away from her. Whatever had struck the two of them had been merciless, unignorable and maybe permanent. Was his sexual need of Cleo the feeling that drove men to propose marriage to women?

The idea was stunning. He'd never given much thought to marriage, though he'd attended weddings of friends and even acted as best man in several.

He got up, absentmindedly brushing the sand from his trunks, a trifle bowled over. It hadn't occurred to him before, but maybe Cleo's reluctance had to do with wanting a husband rather than a lover.

He cleared his strangely clogged throat and looked down at Cleo. "I wish you'd give it a little more time. Moving, I mean. Some more thought."

"I've thought of little else this weekend," she said listlessly. "It's best, Chance."

"For whom?"

Cleo's eyes lifted to his. "For everyone concerned."

"For Rosie?"

Her stare became a glare. "Damn you! Stop bringing her into this. It's between you and me and no one else, particularly her."

In that moment he wanted her more than he ever had. He had to clench his hands at his sides to stop himself from hauling her up off the sand and dragging her into the van. She would melt; she always did. In seconds she would be tearing at his trunks, kissing him wildly, returning every caress, demanding nudity and passion and fulfillment.

But it was broad daylight and they were in a public place. Rosie was playing down the beach with her little friend. Other campers wandered, laughing and talking. A dog barked. Somewhere a radio played.

"When are you returning to the ranch?" he questioned stiffly.

"I'll be back tomorrow afternoon."

"We'll talk again then."

"No, we won't. There's nothing more to talk about."

"Like hell there isn't." His eyes were glittering and his jaw was tight. "We'll talk tomorrow. Count on it." Turning on his heel, Chance strode to the opening in the canvas room and went inside. In the van he peeled away his wet trunks and got into his clothes.

On the beach, Cleo drew up her knees and wrapped her arms around them. Her eyes and nose were stinging with unshed tears. She knew now that she had let herself in for some long-term heartache. Leaving the ranch was sensible, but mere distance wasn't going to destroy her feelings. She would take them with her. Her destination wasn't important; it would be empty and cold. If it wasn't the Kidd River Ranch, it wouldn't be home.

Chance came out, ignored Cleo and trudged down the beach to Rosie. "I'm going, small fry. See you tomorrow, okay?"

"Do you have to go?"

"Yeah, I have to. Today was fun. Keep practicing that stroke and you'll be swimming in the Olympics someday."

Rosie giggled. "You're teasing me."

Chance knelt down. "Yeah, I'm teasing. Give me a goodbye hug."

Cleo saw it all, how her daughter threw her arms around Chance's neck and kissed him on the cheek, and her own heart felt as if it had been shattered into a million pieces.

She got up when Chance came back. "Thanks for teaching Rosie the crawl."

"My pleasure," Chance said. His eyes bored into her. "Come inside the van with me for a few minutes."

"What for?"

"I'd like to prove something to you."

Cleo took a shaky breath. "No."

"Then I'll prove it tomorrow."

"No," she whispered as he walked off, but she knew that he meant it, and knew, also, that he could do it.

It was, after all, the very thing she was planning to get away from.

Early the next morning, Chance and Pete began driving the cows to the loading chute near Nettleton Road. Jim

Candleberry had called on Sunday evening to say he would have trucks there and waiting at 11:00 a.m. sharp.

Chance hadn't slept worth a damn and was in a disgruntled mood. The thought of Cleo coming back from her camping weekend and immediately starting to pack her belongings was like a knife in his gut. He was determined that she not get away without a confrontation, and if it was egotistic of him to have faith in his own powers of persuasion, he really didn't give a damn.

But he'd felt her response too many times to doubt what he did to her. When it happened this time, he angrily told himself, he was going to talk about a future together. Something permanent, by God. If that included marriage in Cleo's mind, well, maybe it was time he took the big step anyway.

One of the cows veered away from the slowly moving herd. "I'll get her," Chance growled, and urged his horse in that direction. The cow headed onto a patch of brushy ground. Chance hadn't yet mastered the art of roping a running animal, but he hopefully swung his rope and gave it a toss.

It fell short and he cussed under his breath. The cow veered again, taking a sharp right turn, and gained some distance. Chance saw the plump birds flapping up from the grass at the cow's intrusion, and judged them to be a variety of grouse. But in the next instant, his horse had also rousted some of the birds. Startled, the horse reared, which caught Chance off guard. He went flying, and landed hard on his back.

He tried to catch his breath and felt an excruciating pain between his shoulder blades. His last thought before blacking out was, *I haven't been thrown from a horse since I was sixteen years old.*

The first thing Cleo noticed when driving into the ranch compound late that afternoon was that the cows were gone. "Candleberry didn't waste any time," she muttered.

"What did you say, Mama?"

"Nothing important, honey." Cleo stopped the van close to her house. Before she could start packing to move, the van had to be unloaded. There were stacks of dirty clothes to wash, and food to carry in to the refrigerator.

She hadn't told Rosie about her plans, which couldn't be put off any longer. "Rosie, don't get out yet. I have to talk to you about something."

The little girl was looking through the windshield at Tisk and Task, who were so happy to see the van, they were running in silly circles. "They're glad we're home, Mama."

"I know, honey, and you can get out and see them in a minute. But..."

"Cleo?"

She turned her head to see Joe hurrying across the compound. Since Joe seldom hurried, Cleo felt some alarm. Getting out, she called, "What is it, Joe?"

"Chance got hurt. His horse threw him and he landed on a rock."

Cleo's heart all but stopped. "How bad is it? Where is he?"

"Pete hauled him to the hospital in Helena."

"He's in the hospital?"

"No, no. Dang it, woman, give me a chance to tell you. The doctor let him come home providin' he stays in bed."

"But he didn't break any bones? Or receive any internal injuries?"

"No breaks. Don't think there're any internal injuries, either, other than his back. He's out of it right now—the doc gave him some pain pills—but he can tell you about it himself when he wakes up."

"Mama?" Rosie tugged on Cleo's arm. She looked down and saw fear in her daughter's eyes. "He's all right, honey. You heard what Joe said. He just has to stay in bed." She looked at Joe. "For how long, Joe?"

"Till he's better, I reckon."

Joe's answer was small comfort. "Where's Pete?"

"Chance sent him over to Candleberry's place. Something about the cows."

Worriedly Cleo glanced to the upstairs windows. She wanted to see Chance with her own eyes, to make sure he really was in one piece. "He's sleeping now?"

"Was a few minutes ago. Go on in, if you want."

"I think I will. Rosie, I need your help." Keeping Rosie busy right now was the best therapy, Cleo decided. "Would you please start unloading the van without me? Start with the refrigerator, honey. There's an empty box in the kitchen. Bring it out and use it to carry the milk and other cold things into the house, all right?"

Rosie nodded. "Can I see Chance, too?"

"Of course you can. When he's ready for visitors, I'll take you to his room. Maybe yet this evening."

"Okay, Mama."

Cleo started for the big house, Joe on her heels. "When did it happen?" she questioned.

"Early this morning. They were bringing the cows down to the loading chute when his horse got spooked by some birds."

"It can happen to the best of riders," Cleo said grimly.

Inside, she proceeded up the stairs alone. Reaching the door to Chance's room, which was ajar, she cautiously pushed it farther open.

He was flat on his back without a pillow. A sheet and light blanket covered him to his waist. His chest was bare, his face peaceful. Cleo thought he looked perfectly normal, as though he were merely sleeping.

Emotion swelled in her chest. He would never be told that she loved him, but she would know it till her dying day. She should escape now, while he was powerless to stop her, while he was too helpless to talk her into anything.

But could she desert the ranch now? True, there was little to do in August without the cows, other than cutting the final crop of hay and eventually moving the steers to lower ground. But she got no pleasure out of visualizing Chance waking up and facing invalidism for an indefinite period without her guidance. He trusted her with the ranch. Through her he could function as nearly normal. He would know the bills were paid on time, supplies bought when necessary, the herd looked after. Maybe Pete could do as well, but it was her whom Chance relied on, not Pete.

She made her decision. She would stay until Chance was on his feet again.

And heaven help her, not a moment longer.

Nine

Chance slept for long stretches because of the powerful pain pills Joe brought him on a regular schedule. When he balked at taking them, Joe crustily argued, "It's the doc's orders, Chance. You can't get better if your pain's so bad you can't rest."

The pain was there, even through the drugged pink haze behind Chance's eyes. During lucid moments he suffered a frustrating sense of helplessness and compared himself to a turtle on its back. It hurt to move anything—his arms, his legs, his head—and he went through the normal array of emotions for an unwilling invalid: anger, self-pity and impatience.

Joe fed him broth, poached eggs and other easily digested foods. Chance occasionally felt hunger, but it wasn't for another cup of broth or an egg, and he suffered drug-induced dreams about juicy steaks and fried chicken.

His dreams weren't all about food. In some he was a boy again, playing with his brothers, or he appeared as a young man in school. His grandfather's image flitted in and out of his consciousness, as did places he'd visited, and people he'd rarely thought about before the accident.

The ranch and the people on it, particularly Cleo, comprised the most persistent theme of his dream. Sometimes he awakened startled to find himself in bed rather than on a horse, and too often he woke up in a sweat because of what he and Cleo had been doing in his dream. Always, during those erotic fantasies, she was malleable and seductive, and beckoning him to a plush, pillow-laden bed that seemed ringed with soft lights and colors.

But those were the dreams Chance liked least. Each one resulted in another bout of frustration. The reality of his situation was a long way from plump pillows and soft lights. Reality was an unknown period of recuperation, unsatisfying food and Joe delivering the bedpan. Dr. Feldman's rigid orders specifically ruled out trips to the bathroom. "You've got badly bruised and torn muscles, Mr. Saxon. Personally I prefer putting you in the hospital, but since you're so adamantly opposed, we'll let you recuperate at home. But you must have total and complete bed rest. I cannot stress enough the importance of immobility at this point."

Cleo came in twice a day, around noon and in the evening. Sometimes Chance was lucid and knew she was there, sometimes he didn't. It bothered Cleo to see him so helpless, and an urge to take care of him herself kept nagging at her. But Joe was doing a good job, and it just wasn't a good idea for her to get that involved. Besides, her time was pretty much taken up with the ranch.

After a few days, by Dr. Feldman's orders, the dosage of pain medication abated and Chance's mind became clearer. He waited that first day for Cleo and was disappointed when she skipped the noon visit. He was staring at the ceiling when she walked in that evening.

Joe had told her downstairs that Chance was alert today, so it didn't surprise her to see his eyes open and his head turning—very carefully—in her direction.

"Hi," she said. "Feeling a little better?"

"Some."

He needed a shave. Cleo thought about offering her services, but every tiny opening between them had resulted in intimacy. Not that Chance was capable of any such shenanigans right now, but he would remember, she knew. If she touched him tonight, he would remember it next week.

"I'm glad you didn't pack up and leave," Chance said.

Cleo perched on the chair near the bed. "I'm planning to stay until you're up and around."

He managed a weak grin. "That could be an argument for permanent disability."

Cleo smiled. "A line doesn't carry much weight right now, so don't waste your strength."

"You talk pretty tough when I can just barely move."

"You're as safe right now as a newborn baby," Cleo said serenely.

"Do you like me better this way?"

Cleo's heart skipped a beat. "Uh...let's just say I don't feel threatened by being in your bedroom tonight."

"And you would if I wasn't all but shackled to this bed?" Chance laughed softly. "You'd have good reason. I might never get enough of you, Cleo."

Her chest tightened. "Let's talk about something else."

"How's Rosie?"

"She keeps asking to see you."

"I'd like to see her, too. Tell her to come by tomorrow. I could use some of her sweet cheerfulness. Anything in the mail?"

Cleo recited the mail deliveries since his accident, and how she had dealt with any that required attention. "You received a letter from John Holby about your credit line application. He merely said that things were moving along and you should receive a yes or no very soon. Everything's under control, Chance. You're not to lie there and worry."

"I'm not worrying. Not with you at the helm. I have been wondering if I should let my brothers know what happened, though."

"Would you like me to call them for you? Not having an extension up here is inconvenient."

"I don't know. I'll think about it a little more. They've got their hands full, and there's not much point in alarming them."

"Just let me know."

"It might not be a bad idea to have an extension installed in this room," Chance said.

"It would be a very good idea. Should I look into it?"

"Please do."

Cleo stood up. "I'd better leave and let you rest. Is there anything you need before I go?"

His eyes moved down her white jeans and back up to her face. He thought of his recent dreams about the two of them, and felt a piercing ache in his loins. "Yeah, there's something I need. Are you willing to give it to me?"

Her cheeks flamed. "You're incorrigible!"

"And you're more potent than pain pills," Chance called out as she vanished through the door. He chuckled, his first one in days, then realized he'd only spoken the truth and there wasn't a damned thing he could do about it. His laugh evolved into a scowl, because he was apt to be all alone in this bed for a good long while.

Chance's recovery was a slow process. By the time he was able to sit up—only with the specific approval of his doctor—Cleo and Pete had taken care of the last hay crop of the season. Fall was just around the corner. Already the nights were cooler. Rosie began talking about the start of the school year during her afternoon visits with Chance; the little girl's happy chatter was always a high point of the long day for him.

Cleo stopped dropping in during the day; evenings were when she caught Chance up with events on the ranch. She sat near his bed and told him every detail of her day and Pete's. A second letter from John Holby announcing the approval of Chance's credit line was related by Cleo without emotion, as was most information. She tried to leave her emotions at home when she came to the big house, since

Chance pounced on anything that sounded remotely personal as quickly as a cat jumped on a mouse.

Though it was taking time, he was gaining strength and mobility every day. He began moving around the second floor, gingerly and without haste. As yet he hadn't tried the stairs, but Cleo could see the end of his infirmity getting closer. She didn't like the idea of Rosie starting school and then changing in midterm, but she simply did not know how to leave the ranch until Chance was fully recovered.

He proved one evening in late August that he was more recovered than she realized. He was lying down, covered with the usual sheet and blanket. He could finally use a pillow again, though not a large one, so he was pretty flat in the bed.

Cleo had been talking about fall roundup and which animals he wished to sell. Chance had closed his eyes, and it took her a minute to realize he must have fallen asleep. Instead of leaving at once, she sat there, silently, and looked at him. He was able to shave himself now, so his jaw was smooth and shiny. His lashes were indecently long, she thought for probably the hundredth time since his accident. *She* should be so lucky.

As for the overall structure of his face, she never tired of seeing it, of admiring it, especially his mouth. No man she'd ever known had such a divine mouth, such a *sinful* mouth. His shock of dark hair, which needed trimming, looked designed for a woman's hands, an experience she had enjoyed several different times during their stormy relationship.

The heat rose in Cleo just from looking at him. The configuration of his body under the blanket was all male, and she knew that body, dammit, *knew* it! Memory blasted her, her own libido blasted her.

She sighed heavily, but continued to sit there and drink in the sight of him. Then, without thinking, she got up from the chair and tiptoed to the bed, where she bent over to smooth the covers. It was a generous impulse for Cleo, as she hadn't gone that close to Chance's bed even one other time since the accident.

His hand snaked out and clamped around her wrist. She yelped. "I thought you were sleeping!" He slid over and pulled her down beside him. "Chance...dammit!"

"Lie still. You don't want to hurt my back, do you?"

"If you were at all concerned about your back, you wouldn't be pulling this trick," she fumed. "Let go of me."

"Tell me lying together doesn't feel good," he murmured huskily.

He was holding on tight, keeping her up against him, her back to his front. "You're not supposed to be lying on your side," she pointed out angrily.

"I've followed that doctor's orders till I'm sick of 'em."

"Chance, Joe could come up here."

"No sale, Cleo. Joe's so glad I can finally make it to the bathroom on my own, he runs out of this house after supper and doesn't show his face until morning." He nuzzled her ear and whispered, "Relax, sweetheart. I won't do anything you don't want."

"You're *doing* something I don't want right now!" Why hadn't she put on jeans after her bath this evening! This was one of those times, worse luck, that she'd needed to get out of constricting pants and into something loose and comfy. A skirt was no barrier at all for Chance when tight jeans barely slowed him down.

He began kissing her cheek, and Cleo was feeling each caress, every movement of his lips. "Please," she whispered. "Don't do this again, Chance. I've tried so hard to resist you."

"Determination only works when there's a lot of space between us, Cleo."

"Don't you think I know that?"

"Turn over and face me. Let me kiss you."

"Chance..." Her voice had a helpless sound. She felt his mouth in her hair.

"You could get away if you really wanted to," he said softly. "Couldn't you?"

"Not without hurting you. Is that what you want, a wrestling match?"

"God, yes," he groaned. "I'd give half the ranch for a good wrestling match with you, sweetheart." His voice dropped to a sensual whisper. "Turn over and face me. Do it because you want to, because you're burning for me, Cleo."

She felt like bawling. Every second in his arms weakened her resolve that much more. How did a woman refuse the man she loved? Even if all he wanted from her was a sexual high, a few minutes of pleasure.

Love was a crock, Cleo thought. What had love for a man ever gotten her, except for Rosie? Even if Chance said right now that he loved her, she wouldn't want to get in any deeper with him.

And yet she couldn't hurt him. Yes, she was strong enough to give him a tussle, and in his condition she'd probably win. But her own conscience wouldn't permit the risk. One false move and he could be back at square one with his damned torn muscles.

But turn over and assist in her own seduction? Never! He could hold her there until dawn and she wouldn't make it easy for him.

Chance's arms were wrapped around her upper body. He could feel her breasts against his forearms, and her bottom was crowded against the blankets covering his lap. He moved his hips and groaned at the bittersweet torment of arousal.

"Get under the blankets with me," he whispered.

"I'm not going to cooperate, Chance, so you may as well forget it."

"You're not? Not even a tiny bit?" One hand dropped lower on her body and began working up her skirt, bunching it at her waist as the fabric gathered there.

She tried to stop the movement of his fingers. "Chance...don't!"

"Let me touch you. If you'd kiss me just once, you wouldn't object to the next step."

"I'm not going to kiss you." But her voice was unsteady and rather ragged. His heat was influencing her, his body next to hers, his voice, everything about him. He should smell like an invalid instead of the sexiest man alive, and he shouldn't *be* so alive in the first darned place!

Finally she just went limp. Chance raised his head slightly. "Are you cooperating?"

"What do you think?"

"Don't try to convince me you don't feel something." He tried to see her face, but holding his head up hurt like hell and he had to let it fall back to the pillow. "Fine, we'll play it your way." He swept her skirt the rest of the way up and slid his hand into her panties.

She squeezed her legs together, but her heart had started racing. He pretended not to notice how tightly her thighs were held and drew lazy circles on her abdomen with his fingertips, while he breathed hotly into her hair. His fingers danced down to her thighs and then clear up to her blouse, where he fiddled with her buttons until one of them gave and he had access to her breasts.

"I can play like this all night," he whispered. "Can you?"

"You're forcing me," she accused.

"I'm what?" His head came up from the pillow.

"Don't play dumb, Chance. You're *forcing* me to lie here!"

The accusation hit home, and the tension in his arms suddenly gave way. "Damn," he muttered. "You really are driving me crazy. Go on, get up."

Cleo sat up and looked at him. "You can make me want you, we both know that. But I'm always sorry after it's over."

"I'm not holding you down now. How come you're not running away?" He sounded bitter, but it didn't prevent him from looking at the swells of her breasts through the narrow opening of her blouse.

Cleo didn't button up, nor did she jump and run. Her blood was rushing through her veins, wild and hot. Her skirt was twisted and up around her hips. He'd teased her into wanting what she knew he could give her so well, without one real kiss or one moment of actual intimacy.

And something was holding her there, making her weigh wisdom against desire. He wasn't well or strong at this moment, but he was still the most potent male she'd ever known.

"No woman wants to be forced," she whispered. "Persuaded maybe, but not forced."

Chance's eyes darkened. "I'm sorry. I apologize. Lie with me, Cleo. Let me just hold you."

Her internal battle was tearing her apart. "We can't keep doing this, Chance. Don't you understand what it does to me? I want to stay and help out until you're well again, but I won't be able to if you grab me every time I come near you."

"I can't seem to stop myself, God knows I've tried. Cleo, I've been thinking about..." For some reason the word *marriage* wouldn't come out of his mouth. He was wild for her, but she had so damned many hang-ups. She still didn't trust him—would she ever trust any man—and would probably laugh if he even hinted at marriage, let alone came right out and proposed. Chance didn't think he could stand having his first proposal to a woman laughed at—especially if that woman was Cleo.

"You've been thinking about what, Chance?"

He disgustedly resigned himself to a sleepless night, or at least a night of unfulfilled, erotic dreams. "It's nothing important. Maybe you should go now. I'm tired."

"Yes, of course." Cleo began buttoning her blouse. Why she suddenly bent forward and kissed him she would never know, but one second she was sitting there and the next her mouth was on his.

His arms came up around her at once, pinning her to his chest. His hungry mouth, wet and hot, devoured hers. His tongue thrust in and out, and his hands skimmed down her back to the tangle of her skirt and under it, seeking bare skin.

He found it. Nearly suffocated from the long kiss and her own inability to breathe normally, Cleo jerked away and scrambled from the bed. With her chest heaving for air, she gasped, "I'm sorry. I shouldn't have done that. Good night."

She was at the door when Chance said hotly, "I never thought you were a tease, Cleo."

"I'm not." She turned. "Or I never was before. I'm beginning to wonder if I ever knew myself at all. Everything I thought I was doesn't seem to have much meaning anymore. I'm either thinking about making love with you or trying to figure out how to rearrange my life so I never see you again. You tell me what it means, Chance. Am I falling in love with you? Sometimes I think so, but I don't like that conclusion so I start the circle all over again."

"Why don't you like that conclusion?"

"Because you're not the man for me. We're as different as day and night. You scare me, Chance, because what passes between us shouldn't happen to a man and woman who don't love each other with every fiber of their being."

"Is any man the right one, Cleo?"

"I don't know that answer, either. I only know that I'm horribly confused. Good night, Chance. If I've upset you, just triple the sensation to learn what you do to me every time you force the issue."

He lay without moving for a long time after Cleo's footsteps died out, pondering love, marriage and Cleo. There was no way a man could want a woman more than he wanted her, but did sexual obsession indicate deeper feelings? How did a man know if he was in the marrying kind of love? How was Cleo feeling when she put him and love in the same thought?

It didn't matter, though, did it? She didn't like the idea. He wasn't the man for her. What did she want, some zombie who never tried to make love to her?

Remembering what she'd said about forcing her stung. At what point did a message of desire become force? Maybe he'd been too "forceful" in every instance with Cleo. It was a serious subject and one he wouldn't forget, although no woman had ever said anything like that to him before.

But then he'd never been so constant in his pursuit of any other woman, either, so driven. Yes, he looked for opportunities to touch Cleo, to kiss her, to make love to her, but was wanting a woman a crime? Especially when her own response proved that she wanted him in exactly the same way?

Cleo wasn't the only person confused in this crazy relationship, Chance thought with some bitterness. This accident and extended recovery period couldn't have come at a worse time for the two of them. She felt stuck at the ranch and he couldn't be so generous as to release her. Maybe that wasn't all bad. Cleo could have been long gone if he hadn't gotten hurt.

But, damn, how could a man court a woman when he could just barely walk?

The next evening Cleo came in with her eyes down. "How are you feeling?"

"Dammit, look at me," he yelled. The day had been eighty hours long and he was so sick of this room, he was on the verge of braving the stairs, with or without Dr. Feldman's permission.

Her eyes jerked up. "Apparently you're feeling like a grouch."

"I'm feeling frustrated, Cleo. Come over here and talk to me."

"Only about the ranch."

"I don't give a damn about the ranch right now. Talk to me about us."

Cleo heaved an exasperated sigh. "Are we going to have another evening like last night? Chance, I don't *want* to talk about us."

"I want to know about Jake. About Rosie's father. What happened eight years ago, Cleo?"

"Nine."

"Eight, nine, what's the difference? Tell me what he did to you."

"I don't want to talk about it."

"No, you'd rather dole out little hints to drive a man off the deep end. Cleo, I have a right to know."

She stiffened. "Based on what, your signature on my paycheck?"

"Can we talk about this without sarcasm?"

"What makes you think you have a right to pry into my life? Because I slept with you?"

"A term I find depressingly inaccurate," Chance drawled.

"Now who's being sarcastic?"

"You're not going to talk to me about Jake."

"No, I'm not. That part of my life is private."

"He hurt you," Chance persisted.

"I guess that's pretty obvious."

"He got you pregnant and ran when you told him."

"Chance, I'm not going to be baited into a discussion, so you may as well drop the subject."

"Aren't you going to sit down?"

"I'm not staying long. There'll be a man from the telephone company here tomorrow to install your extension."

"Took him long enough," Chance said grumpily. His foul mood relented some. "Thanks."

"Maybe when you see your doctor on Monday he'll give you a little more freedom."

"What he'll give me is a back brace and a prescription for physical therapy," Chance said dryly. "The routine's already been explained to me."

"At least you won't be tied to your bed any longer. I'm going now. Get a good night's sleep."

"How?" he shouted as she started through the door.

Cleo stopped to glare at him. "Don't you dare take your bad humor out on me. Instead of wallowing in self-pity, you might remember that you could have been killed by that fall. You were fortunate to only end up with torn muscles, rather than a punctured lung or worse."

"Aw, hell," Chance groaned. "How would you like being stuck in bed for weeks?"

"I'd hate it," Cleo admitted after a moment.

"Maybe you'd be a little self-pitying, too, huh?"

She sighed. His days had to be terribly long, his nights even longer in this empty house. "Probably. Can I bring you anything before I go?"

"Yeah. Bring me yourself."

"*That* attitude is a terrific argument for not coming up here at all! Good night."

Ten

Chance's Monday visit to Dr. Feldman resulted in a little more mobility, but he couldn't drive, couldn't lift anything heavier than a telephone, couldn't ride a horse and had to see a physical therapist in Helena three times a week. He was to stay in bed for at least half of every day, and when he did get up for meals, for walks, or for the trips to the therapist, he had to wear a restricting back brace.

As he couldn't drive, someone had to accompany him to Helena. Sometimes it was Pete, but more often Cleo and Rosie took him in the van.

Cleo was uneasily aware of the deepening relationship between her daughter and Chance. They never ran out of conversation, covering painting with watercolors to what Rosie wanted to do when she grew up. Rosie spoke as naturally and as openly to Chance as she did to her mother. He never patronized the little girl in any way, and he listened to her youthful opinions as though they were pearls of wisdom.

The school year started. Rosie rode a bus from the ranch
to the town of Kidd River, where a large, modern elemen-
tary school educated the town's children and those from the
outlying districts. Rosie loved her school and was thrilled to
return. Cleo was glad, as well, though her reasoning was
much closer to home: A little distance between Rosie and
Chance seemed wise. The child was becoming much too attached to a man she would soon be leaving. Cleo hadn't yet
mentioned the move to Rosie, but the time for a candid discussion was fast approaching. As soon as Chance could
drive, Cleo had decided, she would break all ties with him
and the ranch.

By innuendo, if nothing else, Cleo was kept aware of
Chance's desire for her. Her own feelings bothered her more
than his. She couldn't live out her life in proximity with a
man who wanted her sexually while she struggled with more
important considerations. He could move her sexually, and
he did, with a raised eyebrow, a gesture, a suggestive smile,
a certain tone of voice. But she concealed every response and
kept him at arm's length.

With Rosie in school, however, the trips to Helena immediately proved more difficult. While Cleo drove, Chance
talked, and he had no qualms about bringing up the most
intimate subjects.

"I think about you naked all the time."

"What a dull fantasy," Cleo drawled, though her heart
seemed to turn over. "I would think you could stretch your
imagination much farther than that."

"Ah, but we're not talking about imagination, sweetheart. I've seen and kissed every inch of your beautiful
body, and I have an exceptionally good memory."

"What you have is a dirty mind."

"Only with you, Cleo, only with you."

While Chance was with his therapist, Cleo shopped—
picking up things for Rosie or the ranch—browsed through
bookstores, or merely waited in the van. During the fourth
trip to Helena minus Rosie, a hard storm struck the area.
Cleo was reading in the van, and the rain hitting the vehi-

cle's exterior was suddenly deafening. Outside, the sky looked low enough to touch, dark and ominous, with fierce slashes of lightning.

She watched for Chance, and when she spotted him at the door of the building, she turned the ignition key with the intention of driving closer so he wouldn't get drenched.

The engine sputtered and coughed instead of starting. Frowning, Cleo tried it again. It finally caught and she breathed a sigh of relief. The van had been completely dependable from the day she bought it, and she didn't need it acting up for the first time miles from home in a raging electrical storm.

Chance saw her coming and waited in the building's foyer until the van had stopped in front. Then he turned up his collar and hurried—as much as he could—from the building and got in with a grateful, "Thanks. Where did this come from?"

"The weatherman predicted rain." Cleo put the van in motion, driving slowly in the deluge.

"Yes, but this looks like it could last all day."

"It probably won't, though." Cleo cautiously pulled into the stream of traffic on the street. "The van almost didn't start."

"It seems to be running all right now."

"Yes," Cleo agreed absently. It was raining harder, coming down in sheets, worse than the night she'd run to close the barn door and Chance had been inside. Was it best to wait the storm out in town, or would it pass after a few minutes, as she had indicated to Chance?

By the time they reached the outskirts of the city, the storm's initial fury was diminishing, as Cleo had hoped, although rain continued to fall at a steady rate. It was after two. The school bus dropped Rosie off at three-thirty. Cleo always tried to meet the bus during a storm, as it was a good quarter-mile to the house and she didn't like Rosie getting wet clear to the skin. If they kept going, even slowed down by the weather, she would be at the bus stop in time, Cleo decided.

Halfway to the ranch, however, shortly after making a turn from the highway onto the first secondary road of the trip home, the van's engine began sputtering. What's more, it was raining much harder again.

"Better pull over," Chance said. "If it dies in the middle of the road, someone could run into us in this mess."

Cleo nodded grimly and steered the bucking vehicle to the shoulder.

"There's a side road up ahead," Chance said. "This shoulder is narrow. See if you can make it to that road."

"It sounds like it isn't getting enough gas." Cleo pumped the pedal. The van bucked and coughed during the fifty-yard drive to the side road, but at last they were no longer in danger of being struck by some unsuspecting motorist in the poor visibility. The engine died, and Cleo tried to restart it. "Darn!"

"Cleo, you're only running down the battery. Let it set a while. Maybe it's flooded."

"It wasn't flooded in town. There's something else wrong." Cleo gave it one more try, then turned off the key and sat back. "Now what?" She craned her neck to see the road in both directions, but there wasn't another car in sight. "We could sit here for hours before someone comes along," she said disgustedly before looking at Chance. "Know anything about engines?"

"Not a whole lot," he admitted.

It was a bad idea anyway, Cleo thought. The last thing he should be doing was crawling around in the rain in that back brace. He was making good progress, but one misstep could destroy everything he'd gained from working with the therapist.

But sitting up for too long wasn't good for him, either. "Why don't you get in back and lie down," she suggested. "We could be stuck here until the storm passes."

He looked her right in the eye. "Will you get in back and lie down with me?"

"Dammit, Chance, don't start that again!"

He maintained a level gaze. "How would you prefer I let you know my feelings? You're a beautiful, exciting woman. Intelligent, bright. No one could fault your loyalty or your sense of duty. You're a hard worker and a terrific mother. All of those traits draw me, Cleo, but they wouldn't mean a tinker's damn if you didn't attract me sexually. You refuse to talk about it and get on your high horse every time I try. If I sensed revulsion from you, or dislike, your attitude would be more understandable.

"But I don't repulse you, nor do you dislike me. It's the other way around, in fact. You like me more than you want to, and we both know how in tune we are making love. You're right about one thing, Cleo. As long as you're living on the ranch, or I know where you are, I'm going to pursue you."

Weakly Cleo laid her forehead on the steering wheel. Her heart was thumping, almost as noisily as the rain on the van. She had waged a valiant battle against Chance's determination, but she was only human and becoming weary of the game. Her own body betrayed her constantly. There'd been a few moments since his accident when she'd suffered a massive sense of deprivation and had nearly gone running to him for consolation. There was nothing fun about self-enforced abstinence when the man she visualized herself in love with was not only within reach, but he was also eager to comply and reminding her of his availability at every opportunity.

This was an opportunity. The rain, the stalled engine, the fact that they were once again in her van and away from the ranch and curious eyes. She was dressed for the weather, in jeans, boots, plaid shirt and lined jacket. There was nothing seductive about her appearance, yet he called her beautiful and exciting. Flattery and compliments shouldn't influence her, not in this case, but there was a ring of sincerity in his voice that she was afraid to trust but was too female to ignore.

With her head still on the steering wheel, she turned it slightly to look at him. His eyes were on her, dark blue and containing a brooding circumspection.

"Do you want me to say I love you, Cleo?" he questioned softly. "Would those words make everything all right?"

Her spine tingled. "What you're really asking is, if you said them, would I make love with you."

"Would you?"

"You want an affair, at almost any cost."

"What I want is you. You're the one coming up with labels."

"And if I don't say yes, what will you offer next, Chance?"

"Are you leading up to the subject of marriage, by any chance?"

Cleo's head jerked up. "Good God, I'm not trying to manipulate you into marriage! How could you think such a thing?" Agitated, she crawled from her seat and into the back of the van. There were usually cans of soda in the little refrigerator, and she yanked open the door to get one. "Do you want something to drink?" she asked sharply.

"No, thanks."

Cleo plopped down on the couch rather than returning to the driver's seat. Popping the top on the can of soda, she took a long swallow. "When do you see Dr. Feldman again?"

Chance swiveled on his seat, wincing in the process, to see her. "In about a week. Why?"

"Because this relationship is going to come to a screeching halt the second Feldman says you can drive again. I can't believe you would think I've been leading you on some kind of moronic chase to worm a marriage proposal out of you. That's the biggest bloody insult I've ever received."

"Well, I'm not so sure it's a bad idea."

Cleo's eyes widened. "Marriage? For you and me? Come on, Chance."

"Don't you ever want to get married?"

"It's not something I think about."

"You must've thought about it with Jake."

Cleo looked away. "That was a long time ago."

They were silent until Chance asked, "Are you still in love with him, Cleo?"

"With Jake? Good Lord, no. You sure have a lot of screwy ideas today."

"I've had a lot of time to think lately, Cleo, and since the person I wonder most about won't give me any answers..." He cautiously got out of his seat and stood up, though the van's height wasn't enough to accommodate his and he had to crouch a little. "Maybe I will lie down."

"Are you hurting?" Cleo bounced from the couch to the only other seat in the back, a narrow bench on the opposite wall.

"Yeah, I'm hurting," Chance said dryly, a tone that gave Cleo the idea that he wasn't referring entirely to his back.

While he took off the brace and stretched out on the couch with a grunt of relief, she stretched her boots into the aisle and stared at them, thinking that maybe she didn't give a damn anymore. Chance thinking she was after marriage was absurd, but she had made love with him twice and refused him in between. Maybe an on-and-off attitude in a woman gave a man weird ideas about her motives.

"Lying down feels good," Chance murmured.

Their eyes met across the aisle. Cleo took a slow sip of soda. The rain was almost musical on the roof and left side of the van.

She set down the soda can and shrugged out of her jacket.

Chance's eyes never left her. "What're you doing?"

"It's getting warm in here. Airless." The couch was on the lee side of the van, and she got up and stretched across Chance to crack a window.

"Tempting," he murmured, looking at the underside of her breasts as she leaned forward to reach the window. "Very tempting. Are you doing this on purpose?"

Cleo glanced down at him. "If I opened a window on the other side, rain would come in."

If she hadn't talked about him using force the night he pulled her down to his bed, he would do exactly the same thing right this minute, Chance thought with a muffled groan.

Cleo frowned. "Are you all right?"

His expression became wry. "What do you think? You're leaning over me, and if I make a pass you'll yell 'force' again. A man doesn't know which end is up these days."

Fresh air poured through the inch-wide crack of the window. Cleo took a breath of it and then returned to the bench seat. "Believe me, neither does a woman," she said evenly, as though no time had lapsed between his remark and hers. After enduring his silent stare for a few moments, she got up and moved to the driver's seat to try the engine again.

"It isn't going to start," she said grimly after several attempts. Water was running down the van's windows. The electrical part of the storm had passed, but the rain felt like an all-day, possibly all-night downpour. It was the right time of year for that kind of rainfall, she reminded herself. For that matter, she'd seen rain like this turn to snow after dark and pile up to several feet by morning.

But it wasn't cold enough for snow. All they were going to get was a hell of a hard rain, a dead engine and no traffic. Rosie would either walk home and get drenched or it would occur to Joe to drive down to the bus stop and pick her up. The situation was maddening. Cleo felt helpless and hated it.

Behind her more obvious worries was Chance lying in the back, and the hunger in her own body. Cleo gritted her teeth. Fate worked constantly against her with Chance. Without that fall from his horse, she wouldn't be here and forced to face another decision, another internal battle. She slapped the steering wheel. Why had the van broken down in a damned deluge?

"You might as well relax," Chance said from the couch. "Someone will come along eventually, and you can flag them down. Stewing about it won't make it happen one minute sooner."

"Oh, stop with the fatherly advice," Cleo snapped. "I know the situation better than you do."

Chance slowly sat up. "*Fatherly* advice? Am I that much older than you?"

Cleo wearily rubbed her forehead. "No, of course not. But you sounded patronizing. I'm worried about Rosie." She explained about the bus stop and picking her up during storms.

"I wish I had a solution, Cleo, but other than hiking twenty or so miles to the ranch, I can't think of anything."

"Neither can I," she said on a sigh as she left the driver's seat and returned to the bench in back. "Shouldn't you be lying down?"

"Guess I should." Chance stretched out again, his gaze on the ceiling. "I never thought much about invalidism before this accident," he said. "It's tough. How do you suppose a person copes with a permanent disability?"

"Some people are very courageous, aren't they?" Cleo said by way of agreement.

"They sure are."

Cleo smiled. "Maybe they're better-tempered than you are."

"Hey, I haven't done so bad, considering." Chance chuckled softly. "Maybe you disagree with that."

"I guess you weren't the worst patient in the world." Cleo smiled again. "The second worst, unquestionably, but not the worst."

They fell silent. The interior of the van was warm and cozy. Cleo picked up her soda can and took a sip. "It's getting dark early because of the storm."

"Rosie will be all right, Cleo. Joe or Pete probably picked her up and brought her to the big house. They wouldn't let anything happen to her."

Something in his voice alerted Cleo. "You're worried about her, too. You like Rosie, don't you?" She said it almost accusingly.

"Would you prefer I didn't?"

Cleo hesitated. "Maybe I would. It's going to be hard enough to convince her that moving makes sense without having her upset because she's leaving you."

"She never knew her father, did she?"

"How could she? He thinks I aborted the preg..." Cleo stopped on a shaky breath. "We're not going to start exchanging confidences just because we're caught in a storm together!"

Ignoring her protest, Chance sat up again. "You let him think you were going to have an abortion? Why, for God's sake?"

The decreasing light was blurring Chance's features, but then, Cleo couldn't quite look at him, anyway. Her slip of the tongue required an explanation, like it or not. "He...was married."

"Oh."

"Don't jump to conclusions. I didn't know he was married. He told me about his wife and three children in California after I told him I was pregnant."

"The bastard," Chance said under his breath. "You loved him, didn't you?"

"Yes, I loved him. He said I'd have to get an abortion because he already had a family. I told him I would. I never saw him again."

"And you stopped loving him? Just like that?"

"Just like that," Cleo confirmed flatly.

"Are you going to tell Rosie when she's older?"

"If she asks, yes. She knows her father and I were never married, and I won't lie if she wants further information someday."

"And Jake's rotten tricks put you off men for the rest of your life," Chance said quietly. "Do you think I would do something like that to you?"

"If it suited your purpose, yes."

"When there was a chance you were pregnant, what did I tell you?"

"That you wouldn't desert me."

"Don't you believe I meant it?"

"I don't know if you meant it. It's immaterial, anyway. That's not our problem. Our problem is..."

"What, Cleo. Go on. Our problem is...?"

She cleared her throat. "It's my problem, not yours. I won't gamble with Rosie's future. We've done very well, she and I, and I'd like to keep it at that."

"She won't be eight forever, Cleo. When she's grown and gone, what then? What's in *your* future, Cleo?"

"Not a man," she said flatly.

"I doubt that it's much fun growing old all by oneself."

"Any man who feels that way should find himself a woman to grow old with, by all means."

Chance lay down again and rested the back of one hand on his forehead. "Wouldn't you like to grow old with me, Cleo?"

She gave a short laugh. "I don't think I'm the woman you should start with. There are probably dozens, hundreds of young women out there who are already planning their old age."

"You think this is funny, don't you?"

"What would be funnier is you staying in Montana."

"It keeps coming back to that, doesn't it? *My* background. *My* former life-style. You will not let yourself believe I like it here. Or that I'm staying come hell or high water. Try to comprehend, Cleo. This is my home now. You might be able to go off and forget the ranch, but I never will."

"I'll never forget it, not if I move a thousand miles away! It's been my home for five years. I doubt that you'll be able to say the same five years from now."

"Such disdain for something you refuse to understand," Chance said softly. "Why do you prefer thinking the worst of me? Because I was raised with money? Because I was fortunate enough to receive a good education? Because I've traveled and seen things you haven't? What's the reason, Cleo? You know what I think it is? I think it's because I'm the first man to breach that wall you've got around your feelings. You can't handle feeling anything beyond guilt over an affair with a married man, even though it wasn't your fault. Hate Jake. He deserves it. But don't hate me because of what he did."

"You're very good with words," Cleo said coldly.

"And I'm good in bed, and that's what really turns you upside down. You can't deal with an adult relationship because it makes you *feel*, it makes you come alive and it reminds you of Jake. I think you're still gone on him. That's why no other man can get through to you."

Cleo sucked in a shaky breath. "That's not true."

"Isn't it?"

"No! It hasn't been true for nearly nine years."

Chance's voice dropped. "Then come over here and prove it." When she didn't move, he added, "You can't do it, can you? What's going on in your head right now, Cleo? Are you torn because there's nothing you'd like more than to come over here and yet you're afraid I'll knock down that wall forever?"

"I . . . don't have to prove anything to you."

"Then how about proving something to yourself?"

She was wavering and knew it. If this was merely a line to get her to make love again, it was working. But he'd said so many strange things, like her growing old with him, and that comment about marriage not being a bad idea, and could she still doubt his intentions to stay on the ranch?

The most unnerving result of this conversation, however, was the doubt he'd raised about her feelings for Jake. Since before Rosie's birth she had believed every good thing she'd felt for the father of her baby had died a sudden death. It didn't seem possible that she'd been wrong all this time, especially when she'd been thinking about being in love with Chance. But the question was there now, in her mind, gnawing at raw nerves.

Slowly she slid to the edge of the bench. The light in the van was all but gone. Outside, gray rain and dark skies created a premature nightfall. "What kind of proof do you want?" she asked in a near whisper.

"What kind do *you* want?"

What she wanted was to rip all memory of Jake Hanover from her mind. More than that, though, it seemed crucial to destroy Chance's doubt.

Boldness with a man was alien to her personality. Never had she acted as aggressor or pursuer. Chance had done all the chasing in their topsy-turvy relationship, and before him there'd only been Jake.

She gathered what courage she could and took the two steps across the aisle. Chance scooted over on the couch, and Cleo sat down. They looked at each other in the murky light.

"I feel closer to you than I ever have, Cleo. Do you feel it? Does it seem as right to you as it does to me?"

She wasn't sure the emotions tugging at her should be construed as "right," but for some reason she couldn't say so.

"Maybe holding you is enough right now," Chance said. "Lie with me. In my arms."

She hesitated only briefly. "Yes." She laid on her side so her right arm was across his chest, her head on his shoulder. The tremble in his body caused the same unsteadiness in hers, and she wondered if just holding each other would ever be enough for them. Each ignited something in the other, that much of their bizarre relationship needed no conjecture. It was what she had fought against, right from the first.

Her fight was gone, she realized uneasily. Her vulnerability at this moment was frightening. No man since Jake had gotten this close, either physically or emotionally. Whether Chance knew it or not, he had the power now to destroy her.

His fingers moved on her forearm. "I like this, Cleo," he whispered. "Tell me you like it, too."

"I...like it," she whispered. Was she proving Jake meant nothing by lying next to Chance? Was it even possible to prove such an intangibility to someone else? Her own proof lay within herself, obvious from her quickened pulse, her sensation of breathlessness, the heat curling in the pit of her stomach. She could not feel so much for one man while caring for another.

The doubts about Jake that Chance had created with his in-depth probing had vanished, Cleo realized. She could get off this couch and again feel secure in her version of the past.

But the moment was priceless, a jewel to take out and examine whenever she felt lonely or alone in the future. The life in the man holding her, his warmth, his breathing, his fingers moving on her arm, were too wonderful to forego. Lying with him was the most tenderly moving experience of her life, more powerful than passion, more drugging than desire.

And yet passion was present, simmering below the surface of calmer thoughts. Desire was stirring, making her blood run faster, her heart beat harder. She could feel a clenching in Chance's arms around her, a message of arising need.

She tipped her chin up, he tipped his down. Their eyes met, his dark and hopeful, hers deep green and compliant. His mouth brushed hers, then the tip of his tongue moved slowly across her lips. She trembled, he shuddered. "Cleo..."

"I hear you," she whispered.

His hand moved to her breast and caressed it through her clothing, hers pulled his shirt from his jeans to go under it. They kissed, a slow mating of mouths that had them gasping and straining together.

He opened the button on the waist of her jeans and then the zipper. She undid his belt and fly. His hand went into her jeans, her hand went into his. Their kisses became hungry, greedy.

Then he groaned. "My back."

She sat up. "Lie still. Let me do the work."

His eyes glittered. "Gladly."

She unbuttoned his shirt and pushed it open. Her mouth moved over his bare chest, nipped at his throat, at his nipples. His eyes had closed, she saw, and the expression on his handsome face was one of supreme pleasure.

She wanted him inside her, desperately. He couldn't do it, but there was nothing wrong with her back. She got off the couch. His eyes opened to see her pushing down her jeans.

At that tension-filled moment the sound of an approaching vehicle intruded. Cleo's startled eyes locked with Chance's. "Someone's coming."

Chance emitted a groan of utter agony. Cleo darted to a window. "It's Pete!" Quickly she dragged up her jeans and straightened her shirt. She grabbed her jacket, her gaze falling on Chance's lap. Her heartbeat was so erratic and she felt so flushed, Pete was apt to suspect something from her alone. But Chance's arousal was indisputable proof of their misbehavior. "Do something," she pleaded. "Fix your clothes."

He sat up and zipped himself into his jeans. "Will you come to the house tonight?"

"I . . . don't know."

"We're hanging, Cleo, both of us. We made great headway today. Don't regress because we were interrupted. Say you'll come to the house tonight."

She heard Pete's pickup come to a stop outside. "We can't talk now." She went to the side door of the van and pushed it open. "Hi, Pete."

"Hi, yourself. What happened? Joe and me were gettin' worried. Thought I'd better drive to Helena in case there was a problem."

Cleo jumped to the ground. "There is. The van broke down. Is Rosie all right?"

"Joe met her bus. She's fine."

Cleo looked up at the sodden, dark sky and felt a light drizzle on her feverish face. The rain was a mere trickle compared to its previous intensity.

"Is Chance okay?" Pete questioned.

"He's been lying down. Chance, let's go home," she called into the van.

Eleven

Chance felt a slow-burning anger. Cleo was avoiding him, speaking to him only when she couldn't get out of it. After the progress they'd made during the storm, he'd expected better than that from her.

All he could think of was her, of how she'd started to undress in the van to make love to him, and what would have happened if Pete hadn't come along at precisely the worst possible moment.

He was so fed up with semi-invalidism he found himself wishing for the money to go somewhere. Anywhere. The approved credit line with the Helena bank taunted him, because obtaining the money to escape the doldrums for a while would be as easy as picking up the telephone.

But then there would be a mortgage on the ranch, and when he came back from wherever, nothing would have really changed except for an unnecessary debt.

Chance stood at the study window and stared out at the bleak landscape. The recent storm had been a forerunner of bad weather. The temperature had been hovering in the high forties ever since, even when the sun intermittently penetrated the heavy cloud cover.

This is reality, he thought broodingly. Very little money, a bad back and lousy weather. Never had he been faced with a long winter and frustration because it took money to eradicate boredom. Money or someone exciting. Cleo could be that someone, but after the other day, or rather the other evening, when he'd waited for her to come to the house and she hadn't, he'd finally admitted the futility of his feelings for her. Cleo relented one step and backed up two. No man could live with that kind of ambivalence forever.

So, he'd like to go somewhere, maybe to Nevada to see Rush, or Oregon to see Cash. Those trips wouldn't cost much if he drove and watched costs. Chance grimaced. When in hell was Dr. Feldman going to give him the green light on driving a car?

"Chance?"

He turned and kept his expression impassive, although, as normal when he was near Cleo, things started happening with his body. "Yes?"

"I've talked to Pete. He'll be driving you to Helena for your appointment with your therapist. He'll be along in a few minutes."

"Fine," Chance said stonily. The van was running again, merely a clogged fuel line. Cleo could drive him, but he'd suspected she would make other arrangements. Her attitude infuriated him. They could have something special and she wouldn't allow it, even though he had a lot of proof that she wanted it as much as he did.

Then again, he also had a lot of proof that she didn't. That's what had him symbolically climbing the walls, the way she could run so hot and cold on him.

Cleo had barely stepped into the room. She turned to go, then stopped. "Do you remember me telling you about Pete being gone for a few weeks?"

"I remember. Is that coming up?"

"Next week. His vacation time. I just wanted to remind you."

"Thanks."

Cleo drew a breath. She wasn't especially glad that Pete had come along when he did during the storm, but it had been best. Chance's dissenting opinion was all too obvious, however, and she wished she knew what to say to him to make him understand her point of view. Sometimes people behaved out of character. The storm had been influencing, as well as Chance's glibness. She would not put herself in that position with him again, and if Pete was unavailable to chauffeur him to Helena, then Joe would have to do it.

"I have work to do. See you later," she said quietly.

"What work?"

Again Cleo stopped. "Right now I'm cleaning the tack room."

"You never run out of chores, do you?"

"My doing my job makes you angry?"

Chance couldn't choke it back any longer. "*You* make me angry. I'm surprised you braved coming in here, the way you've been avoiding me."

Her own thoughts surprised her, or rather, what she was picking up from Chance. "You're ready to let me leave the ranch now, aren't you?"

He hadn't thought of his foul mood in that light, but she wasn't wrong. She was a constant burr, a point of irritation. Her long, denim-clad legs made him ache more than his injured back did, and her green eyes haunted his dreams.

"If you want to go, go," he said flatly. "It's up to you."

The sudden pain in Cleo's system was nearly unbearable. She'd threatened and promised to leave so many times, but never had she imagined him being so cold about it.

Her voice came out emotionless. "Consider it done." Whirling, she walked away.

Chance stood there, ice-cold and hurting. He raised his hand and ran his fingers through his hair, thinking absently that he needed a haircut. *Consider it done.* When would she go? Today, tomorrow, next week? Rosie's sweet face came to mind, and he realized that he would miss the little girl almost as much as her mother.

He swore, quietly but efficiently. Falling in love brought nothing but misery to a man.

The thought brought him up short. He *was* in love with Cleo, dammit, and he didn't have to ask himself how he knew, either. It was as obvious as the nose on his face. He loved her, and he'd practically said right out that he couldn't care less if she walked out of his life and never looked back.

He paced for a few minutes, torn by opposing emotions. He didn't feel wrong about taking a stand with Cleo, but he kept thinking how lonely the ranch would be without her and Rosie.

Finally he grabbed the jacket he'd hung over a chair and pulled it on, then walked through the house with more speed than he'd mustered in a long time.

Brushing the tears from her eyes, Cleo strode to the barn and went into the tack room. She looked around and remembered that cleaning it was no longer her job. The hurting inside of her erupted in anger, and she kicked at a saddle, knocking it from its stand.

She left it where it fell, and deserting the tack room with its aroma of leather and horses, headed for her house. Inside, she tossed her hat and jacket, and yanked the pins from her hair. Finger-combing it back from her face, she tried to organize her benumbed brain. Rosie was in school right now. Not only would she have to be told about the move, the school would also have to be notified. Packing would take several days. Were there any empty boxes on the ranch? A truck would have to be hired, and two men to load her furniture.

The front door opened. Cleo's eyes widened at the sight of Chance walking in. Her greeting wasn't at all friendly. "What do you want?"

He closed the door. "A showdown."

"I think we already had that."

"What we've had are fights, arguments, debates and the greatest sex a man and woman could ever attain. But, no, Cleo, we've never had a showdown."

She swung around and left him standing near the door while she moved into the living room. "Well, we're not having one now, either."

Following, Chance's gaze swept what he could see of the house. It was tiny but spotlessly clean and nicely decorated. "I've never been in here before."

"You were never invited." Cleo pointed this out coldly. Him being here was unnerving. He was too big for this room. His head practically touched the low ceiling, and his shoulders were easily as broad as her largest chair.

He seemed broader than when he arrived, she thought then, though she would swear he hadn't put on any weight. He looked much different than the day she'd come up on him checking the rock wall of the big house. His hair was longer, his skin darker, his jeans more faded, his boots not quite as shiny. He looked like a working rancher now, even to the completely masculine expression in his incredibly blue eyes.

It was suddenly difficult for Cleo to breathe. He was too handsome, too sexy, and she could smell his scent in the tiny room. She nervously smoothed her hair. "I don't want another argument."

"A showdown isn't an argument."

"You told me to go, and . . ."

"I changed my mind."

"It's not your decision!"

"I'm making it mine." He took a step toward her, and then another.

She felt hunted, stalked, and she backed up until the arm of the sofa pressed into her legs. "I can only guess at what you're thinking right now, but it's undoubtedly best if I don't know. Please leave."

"Forget that notion. Remember when we talked about proving things?"

"Of course I remember! Don't think that a few confidences give you any . . ."

"I'm going to prove something to you, Cleo, and after I do, we're going to talk."

"No," she gasped.

He took off his jacket and dropped it on a chair.

"Chance..." Her heart was running wild. She could see he wasn't wearing his back brace, so he'd either left the house in haste or with something in mind. She suspected it was a little of both. "Joe will wonder what you're doing in my house. Pete will be looking for you."

"Let them both wonder." He put his hands on her shoulders. "Do you actually think I give a damn what anyone might think about me being here?"

Cleo stared into his eyes. He was sinner and saint, all in one irresistible package, and he kept testing her, taking her to and then beyond her own self-imposed limits. Her legs had become rubbery, and she felt herself weakening, being emotionally drawn to him against her will.

Someone rapped on the front door and called, "Chance? Cleo?"

"It's Pete," Cleo whispered. "Your appointment."

Chance tensed. "Tell him to go away."

"No. You have to go."

He yanked her forward and kissed her, hard and hot. Cleo reeled when he let go of her and went to the chair for his jacket. "We'll finish this when I get back." He paused at the door for one more look at her, then pulled it open. "I'm here, Pete. I've got to stop at the house for my brace before we leave."

Cleo sank onto the sofa. Enough is enough, she thought with a low moan. He wanted her to go, he wanted her to stay. What *she* wanted, needed desperately, was some time to sort it all out. It was Friday. When Rosie got home from school, she could leave for the weekend. She was *not* going to be here when Chance got back.

Forcing calmness on her overwrought system, Cleo got up and walked to her bedroom. She put a few things into a suitcase, then went to Rosie's room to gather what would be needed for a weekend.

* * *

Chance spotted the van missing before Pete parked his truck. First disbelief, then anger rocketed through him.

"Looks like Cleo went somewhere," Pete remarked.

"Yes," Chance agreed through clenched teeth. He got out and stalked into the house. "Joe, did Cleo say where she was going?"

"I didn't even know she was gone."

Great, just great. Chance continued through the house to the stairs. His back was hurting and he needed to lie down. With the brace off, he stretched out on the bed, but he listened for the sound of the van returning instead of relaxing.

He heard nothing, except for Joe moving around on the first floor. It's over, he thought after a while. A man could chase after a woman only so long; he'd done everything he knew how, and it was time to call it quits. Obviously Cleo had left the ranch to avoid what he'd promised, to finish what he'd started when he got back from Helena.

She would have no reason to worry ever again. She could come, go or stand on her head, and he wouldn't react, not so she'd notice, at any rate. He'd played the fool long enough.

To make the weekend special for Rosie, Cleo chose a motel with an indoor swimming pool. They swam and played in the heated water for an hour, then went to their room and ordered hamburgers and fries from room service. Rosie thought spending the weekend in a motel was "cool," especially since her mother allowed her to watch TV while she ate.

Cleo picked at her food while Rosie giggled over the antics of some cartoon characters. When the program ended, Cleo got up and switched off the set. "You may watch again later, honey. I need to talk to you for a few minutes."

"Sure, Mama." Rosie plunked the last fry on her plate into her mouth.

Cleo perched on the edge of the bed and looked at her little daughter, who was still sitting at the small round table. "How would you like to live in a town, honey?"

"A town?" Rosie echoed with a mystified expression. "What town, Mama?"

"Well, I haven't decided that yet. But we're going to move away from the ranch, Rosie."

Rosie's eyes got huge. "How come?"

"There are several reasons," Cleo replied. "Grown-up reasons. Rosie, I've never once said to you that you were too young to understand anything. I've always answered your questions to the best of my ability, and I always will. But explaining my reasons for leaving the ranch so you would completely understand would be very difficult." Cleo paused to begin again. "It mainly has to do with you and me, honey, and what I feel is best for us. Can you accept that?"

Rosie wore a perplexed frown. "But what about Chance? And Joe and Pete? Would we visit them?"

"Uh . . . possibly."

"I don't think Tisk and Task would like living in a town, Mama," Rosie said solemnly.

Cleo gulped. She'd forgotten about the dogs. In fact, she'd forgotten them so completely, she'd driven away today without talking to Joe about them. Whenever she left the ranch, she brought dog food to Joe so he could feed Rosie's pets. Today Tisk and Task hadn't crossed her mind.

It was quite likely, she realized uneasily, that the little dogs were hungry right now and no one would think to look after them, not when she had gone off without a word.

Another aspect of owning two active pets was also hitting Cleo. Wherever she went she would have to rent, and if she remembered correctly, a good many landlords objected to pets. Particularly *two* pets.

"Maybe Tisk and Task would be happier staying at the ranch," she said quietly.

Rosie looked horrified. "But they would get lonesome for me!"

The subject was upsetting Cleo as well as Rosie. Why hadn't she thought of the dogs before talking about moving to her daughter. Naturally Rosie wouldn't want to leave her best friends behind. And there was Cleo's horse, Midnight, to consider, also. How could she have overlooked the animals?

Most crucial at the moment, however, was making sure someone at the ranch fed Tisk and Task today. Pete would take care of Midnight along with the other horses, but she had to do something about the dogs.

Cleo got up from the bed and bent over Rosie to kiss her cheek. "We'll talk more about it later. I have to make a phone call. Would you like to watch TV again?"

Rosie nodded, but Cleo could see that much of her daughter's excitement over staying in a motel with a swimming pool and a color TV had faded.

Cleo switched on the set and then clicked through the available channels to find a program she thought suitable for an eight-year-old. Satisfied with a family-oriented situation comedy, Cleo left Rosie to herself and walked over to the bed stand, which contained the telephone.

She sat on the bed and picked up the phone, hoping that Joe was still at the house and would answer. But it was Chance who said, "Kidd River Ranch," into her ear.

Her mouth went dry. "Chance? This is Cleo." All she heard was silence. "Uh...I'm calling to ask a favor of someone. I went away and forgot to bring dog food to Joe to feed Tisk and Task. I just now thought of it," she finished lamely.

"I'll take care of it."

"I'm sorry to even ask. The dogs are my responsibility, and I drove off without..."

"I said I'll take care of it."

He sounded as distant as the stars, as though they were two strangers. Cleo clutched the phone in a death grip, realizing that she had finally attained what she'd so diligently insisted upon—Chance's disinterest.

"Well...thank you," she said in a strained whisper. "Goodbye."

"Goodbye."

Numbly she put down the phone. Behind her, Rosie giggled about something on TV, and the program itself was filled with wisecracks and laughter. Something had just gone out of Cleo's life, and the ensuing void felt as large and vacant as a crater. She got up and went into the bathroom for a drink of water, and then stood in the glare of bright lights on white tile and looked at her ashen reflection in the mirror.

Chance hadn't asked where she was or when she would be back. He hadn't berated her for leaving without telling someone, nor accused her of thoughtlessness. He'd sounded neither angry nor friendly... just disinterested.

Cleo's hand rose to cover her mouth, but holding back a moan didn't stop hot tears from filling her eyes. She had exactly what she had demanded from Chance all along, and it didn't feel at all as she'd planned.

She cleared her throat and called, "Rosie? I'm going to take a shower," and heard in return, "Okay, Mama." Then she closed the bathroom door, turned on the shower and let her tears turn to sobs.

Twelve

Cleo collected a supply of cardboard boxes—all she could cram into the van—before leaving Helena on Saturday. Initially she had planned to be gone through Sunday, but the flavor had gone out of the weekend. Rosie was uncommonly subdued during the drive home, and Cleo knew that her daughter's uncharacteristic silence was due to the upcoming move. Hiding her own sense of dangling somewhere in outer space, she tried singing their favorite songs and instigating games, but Rosie's participation was apathetic, at best.

When they arrived at the ranch, Rosie jumped out of the van and called for her dogs. Cleo sighed. She didn't like moving any better than Rosie did, but what else could she do now? Ordinarily she would have requested that Rosie help unload the boxes, but today she let her play.

She carried several boxes into the house and stacked them in the living room. On her third trip, Joe appeared with a disgruntled expression. "What in heck you doin'?"

Gripping two large boxes, Cleo stopped. "Didn't Chance tell you?"

"Tell me what?"

"I'm moving, Joe."

Joe looked thunderstruck. "You're leaving the ranch?"

"Yes." Cleo continued into the house, with Joe trailing right behind her. She put the two boxes with the others. "I'm surprised Chance didn't say something."

"You ain't quittin' your job, are ya?"

"Afraid so, Joe."

"Well, how come you'd go and do something like that?"

Cleo sighed. "It's a long story, Joe."

"It sure beats all," he said grumpily. "Chance ain't saying two words to anyone, now this."

"He's not?"

"He's been as grouchy as a bear with a toothache all day." Joe's pale blue eyes narrowed. "Got somethin' to do with you leaving, I'd be willin' to bet."

"I doubt it." Cleo walked away, aware of Joe tagging along. Outside at the van, she handed him some boxes, which he carried in. With his help, the van was unloaded in short order, and the big pile of boxes in the living room blocked passage to the sofa and chairs.

"Won't be doing any sittin' in here," Joe observed dryly from the doorway.

"No," Cleo agreed. "Joe, when Pete comes in for supper, would you tell him I'd like to talk to him sometime tomorrow?"

"Why'nt you come to the house and tell 'im yourself?"

"I'd just rather not. Will you tell him?"

"Yeah, I'll tell 'im," Joe said without bothering to conceal his disgust. "Doggone, but you and Chance are stubborn cusses. What're you gonna do, pack up and git without speakin' a word to him?"

"Uh . . . no. I'll have to see him before I leave." She had a paycheck coming, and a ring of keys that belonged to the ranch. There was the matter of Midnight to discuss, as well.

Cleo planned to ask Chance if her horse could stay on the ranch until she found a place to board him.

Joe left with his face screwed up in an unmistakable scowl of disapproval. Cleo stood at her front door and watched Rosie and the dogs for a few moments, then sighed and went back inside.

She wondered where to begin with the packing, which room, what items. Squeezing into the living room, she picked up some framed snapshots from a small table, mostly of Rosie, then decided that was as good a place as any to start. Using old newspapers for wrapping, she began filling a box.

"Mama, can Tisk and Task sleep in the house tonight?" Rosie asked after her prayers had been said.

Sitting on Rosie's bed to tuck her in for the night, Cleo smoothed her daughter's dark curls from her forehead. "They like sleeping in the barn, honey."

"How do you know?"

"Don't you remember when you brought them in a few weeks ago? Didn't they wander and bark and ask to be let out?"

Rosie yawned. "Maybe they chase mice in the barn."

"Maybe they do."

"Mama, are we going to leave them here when we move?"

Cleo drew a slow breath. "I've been trying to figure out where they would be happiest, Rosie. What do you think?"

"Will our house in town have a yard?"

"We might be living in an apartment for a while, honey. Do you know what an apartment is?"

"It's a big house with lots of rooms."

Cleo smiled. "With lots of different families. I'm going to try to locate a house just for us, but sometimes vacant rental houses are hard to find."

"Tisk and Task wouldn't like an apartment, would they?"

"I don't think they would. They're very happy running all over the ranch."

"Chance lets them run anyplace they want."

"Yes, he does."

"Mama, are we going to like an apartment?"

Cleo bent over and kissed her daughter's soft cheek. "We'll try, okay? Sleep well. See you in the morning."

"Good night, Mama. See you in the morning."

After snapping off the lamp and leaving Rosie's door ajar, Cleo went to the kitchen. A large box was waiting on the table, half-filled. Cupboard doors were hanging open. The little house was being torn apart, and to Cleo it felt as if she was being torn apart, as well.

She brushed away a tear, reminded herself that her choices had disappeared and got to work. But packing kitchen utensils didn't require much brainpower, and she kept thinking about everything that had happened since Chance's surprising arrival.

Obviously she'd been wrong about his longevity, summer was over and he was still here. Chance's plans for the ranch swirled in her mind. Since her employment, the operation had changed very little—until Chance had arrived. He was changing it, drastically. The place seemed almost vacant without the cows, though the steers he hadn't sold still added up to a nice herd. Maybe change was what the place had needed, she mused in her disquietude. Certainly it hadn't been showing much profit from old routines.

Cleo tried to elude the more painful memories while she worked, those moments with Chance that had nothing to do with the ranch. Those times lived in her mind with a stubborn tenacity, however, and kept rising to the forefront of her thoughts. Whatever else happened in her life, she knew she would never forget this summer with Chance. He had made her question her own stringent ethics and wonder about love, when she'd done neither for many years. Her objections to the relationship were rooted in fears from the past, she knew that, but even now, filling boxes with her and

Rosie's possessions and quaking internally because their future seemed so shaky, she couldn't relent.

Besides, Chance no longer wanted her. He'd made that glaringly clear on the phone Friday evening, and from his complete silence since she got back.

Pensive, Cleo skirted boxes and walked to the front door, which she opened for a breath of fresh air. It was getting late, after eleven. The air contained the piercing night chill of the fall season in this high country. The big house was dark, as was the bunkhouse. Joe's trailer couldn't be seen from the compound, tucked as it was within a stand of cottonwoods in a crook of the Kidd River a half mile away.

Cleo stepped into the yard and looked up at the sky, which had the appearance of the encroaching winter—long, thin clouds, a sharp, clear half-moon. Her gaze moved to the second-story windows in the big house, to the one she knew was Chance's. Was it possible he was standing in the dark room looking at her?

It was an inane thought. Impatient with her imagination, Cleo turned to go in. An eerie red glow in the barn caught her eye, and she stopped to peer at it. It took a second, but then she knew what it was. "Fire!" she shrieked, and took off running toward the barn, screaming, "Chance! Pete! The barn's on fire!"

Chance stirred. Someone was yelling. He came awake slowly. The shouts were noisy but unintelligible. Frowning, trying to grasp what was going on outside, he pulled himself up, automatically using the method of changing positions taught him by his therapist. Then Cleo's voice registered, and he moved more quickly, sliding off the bed, hurrying to the window.

The compound was dark. He looked for Cleo and couldn't see her. But then he stopped looking, because he saw the flames coming through the roof of the barn.

"My God!" Hastily he turned on a light and searched for clothes, a pair of jeans, his boots without socks, a shirt left unbuttoned. Racing downstairs, he hit the back door running. "Cleo!"

She was dragging a long hose. "Chance! I'm down here."

He forgot his back and ran. Pete was running, as well. Cleo got the hose attached to the corral spigot just as they ran up. Pete latched onto the other end of the hose and shouted, "Turn it on!"

Cleo had already done so, and the water came gushing out. She saw Chance heading into the barn and shrieked, "Chance!"

"He went after the horses," Pete yelled. "There're two locked in stalls."

"Keep the water on the door!"

Smoke billowed out of the barn from every opening. In the few minutes since Cleo had spotted the red glow, the fire had evolved into voracious, crackling, roaring flames, a horrifying sound she'd never before heard.

And Chance was in there. Cleo stood there, frozen with fear, trembling as though caught by a high wind.

"Mama! Mama!"

Cleo whirled. Barefoot and in her pajamas, Rosie leaped into her arms. She held her daughter for a moment, then released all but her hand. "Go back to the house, Rosie."

"But, Mama..."

She heard Pete yelling. "Here comes the horses! Watch 'em, they're panicked and running wild!"

Cleo pulled Rosie out of the way, her gaze riveted on the door. She nearly collapsed with relief when Chance stumbled out. Benumbed, she let Rosie's hand slip from her grasp without realizing it.

The little girl streaked away. "Chance! Chance! Tisk and Task are in the barn!"

Cleo shouted, "No, Rosie!" She ran for her daughter, but Rosie was crying and clinging to Chance's leg.

Chance unhooked her fingers. "Stand back, Rosie. Pete, wet me down."

"No!" Cleo cried. "You can't go back in there."

"There's no time to argue. Get back or get wet! Pete, turn the hose on me!"

Wild-eyed, Cleo dragged Rosie away from the spraying water. At the last minute, while Chance was running for the barn door, she shouted, "They've been sleeping in the tack room!"

Pete was doing the best he could with one small hose, but Cleo could see the barn was a lost cause. Tears dripped down her face. Rosie sobbed into her leg and Cleo tried to soothe her daughter by stroking her hair.

But her heart and soul were with Chance in that burning barn, risking his life to save Tisk and Task. Her own sobs melded with Rosie's, and she prayed with passion, with promises, with every fiber of her being.

The awful minutes seemed like an eternity. Cleo felt her legs nearly giving out when Chance came through the door with a dog under each arm. Rosie shrieked, "He did it, Mama! He saved Tisk and Task!"

A safe distance from the barn, Chance lowered the dogs to the ground. The pair, smoky and sooty and barking, ran unerringly to Rosie, who knelt in the dirt and scooped them into a hug. Cleo walked over to the happy trio. "Take them to the house, Rosie. And stay there, honey." Her voice had no power, she realized, barely a thread of its normal strength.

Chance walked up. His skin and clothing were layered with soot and grime. Rosie stood up and threw herself at him. "Thank you, Chance, thank you, thank you!"

"You'll get dirty hugging me, honey," he said, and Cleo could tell there wasn't much strength in his voice, either.

"Thank you," she said huskily. "What you did ... I'll never forget it."

"Everyone's safe, that's what matters." Chance turned to Pete. "Might as well turn off the water, Pete. The barn can't be saved."

It was coming down fast. The roof caved in, sending up an immense shower of sparks. Cleo held back a sob. Chance was right: Everyone was safe, and that's what mattered.

She looked down at her little girl. "Take the dogs and go to the house, Rosie. You're cold and barefoot."

"All right, Mama. Come on, Tisk and Task," she called, and took off running.

Pete came over to stand by Chance and Cleo. "What d'ya suppose caused it?"

Chance shook his head. "Who knows, Pete? Maybe the insurance adjuster will figure it out." He thought about money and sent a prayer heavenward that the building was insured. "We'll build a new barn."

Cleo's heart wrenched. Chance *was* here to stay, already planning to build a new barn. She'd been so wrong about him, so terribly, heartbreakingly wrong. He'd given her every kind of hint a man could, asking her if she wouldn't like to grow old with him, suggesting that marriage wasn't a bad idea. And she'd cut him off at the knees again and again, until finally she destroyed his feelings for her.

The three of them stood there and watched the barn burn, until the heat of the fire no longer reached them and the cold of the night made them shiver.

"Might as well go in," Chance said. "Thanks, Pete. You gave it your best." He turned to Cleo as Pete walked off. "Thanks, Cleo."

"I did very little."

"You did what you could. That's what we all did."

"You did much more," she whispered raggedly. "Not too many men would risk their own life to save a little girl's pets."

"Well...I don't know about that. I can't see anyone with any compassion standing around and not trying." He saw her paleness, the exhaustion on her face. "It's over, Cleo. Go to bed. You look done in." He took her arm. "Come on. I'll walk you to your house."

She could smell the smoke in his clothing, his sweat, and the grimy hand on her arm felt like utter security. If she could only go back and do it all again, she thought sadly. Why didn't a person recognize something wonderful before it was too late?

At the gate, she thanked him again. But there wasn't anything else to say. The night was silent again. Only some glowing embers in the distance remained of the once proud barn. She went in and closed the door of the tiny house behind her, then pushed through the boxes in the living room to reach the front window to watch Chance go into the big house.

Her anguish was richly deserved, she thought unhappily. She was a fool, and fools didn't deserve anything else. Why she'd thought it necessary to threaten a break with the ranch every time Chance had upset her was beyond reason. The only things she'd done since his arrival to raise any self-pride were the times he'd infiltrated her defenses enough to reach her better side. Everything else was a fiasco, completely ridiculous and horribly painful to remember.

When there was nothing left to see outside, Cleo deserted the window and went to Rosie's room. The little girl was sound asleep, with Tisk and Task, those dirty little scamps, snuggled in bed with her. Allowing the dogs on furniture was against all rules, but tonight the sight brought Cleo some comfort. She smiled weakly, finally facing that she couldn't separate Rosie and her pets. Wherever she and Rosie ended up, Tisk and Task would be with them. Sighing, Cleo went on to the bathroom for a shower before going to bed herself.

Wearing a nightgown ten minutes later, a glance at the clock surprised her. Only two hours had passed since she'd first seen the fire, two measly hours that felt like two weeks. She shuddered over the memory of Chance going into the burning barn, not once but twice. He could be horribly injured right now, or worse, dead.

Groaning, Cleo turned off the light and crawled into bed. But falling immediately to sleep wasn't possible. Her nerves were jumping around like popcorn in a hot skillet. She couldn't stop thinking of Chance, and how cruelly she'd treated every one of his advances. He hadn't stopped trying, though, not until this weekend. Had he truly lost every feeling for her? Or was he just so disgusted with her constant denials that he'd simply given up?

Cleo's heart began beating faster. She had to see him before she left the ranch for business reasons, but how would he react if she went to him right now? To his room? He'd invited her, several times, but this was different. She'd be going without an invitation or any assurance of welcome. He might tell her flat out to stay out of his life, or maybe think she'd gone off the deep end.

But hadn't she? In a way? By tomorrow night everything in the house would be packed. On Monday she would pick up Rosie's school records. Things were coming to a head very quickly. If she procrastinated with this, she would find herself driving away from the ranch and never seeing Chance again. That idea had her throwing back the covers and starting out of bed.

Then she thought of Rosie. With her heart in her throat, Cleo lay down again. She couldn't go to Chance now. They had all come close to tragedy tonight, and she wouldn't forget for a moment that Rosie was alone in the house and sleeping. When she talked to Chance, her mind couldn't be on Rosie's safety. She had to be clearheaded, lucid, and it probably wouldn't hurt if she didn't look as though she'd just taken a shower and gone to bed with wet hair. Which was only the truth, of course, but how would limp, damp hair and sunken eyes from lack of sleep help her case?

Cleo did get up, but it was to gulp two aspirin tablets, not to go to Chance.

She would see him in the morning.

Rosie was awed by the charred debris of the barn. "It's all gone, Mama."

"Fires are terrible things, Rosie." Cleo looked down at her daughter. "How would you like to visit your friend Darcy today?"

Rosie's face lit up. "Really?"

"I called her parents and they would love to have you come and play with Darcy. I'll drive you over."

"Right now?" Rosie asked excitedly.

"Right now."

"I'll get my dolls, okay?"

"Run and get them. I'll wait in the van." Cleo knew Joe's Sunday routine like the back of her hand. He came to the big house, fixed breakfast, put a big beef roast, a ham or a turkey into the oven on low heat for supper and left the ranch to play pinochle with his friends in Kidd River. Pete's routine was not quite so predictable. Sometimes he worked, sometimes he merely hung around the bunkhouse, occasionally he went somewhere.

But, by the same token, Pete rarely entered the house outside of mealtimes. Pete would not be a deterrent to conversation with Chance, which was what Cleo hoped for from the day. There were no speeches lined up in her head, but ideas, apologies and a need for honesty were tripping over each other.

The round-trip to drop Rosie off at her friend Darcy's home took an hour. Cleo parked the van near her house again and hurried inside for the final preparations, which were so well planned, she saw to them quickly. Bathed, with her hair loose and curled slightly, wearing makeup and cologne and what she considered her prettiest fall outfit—a slim black skirt, a white silk blouse and black leather pumps—she told her racing pulse to slow down and left the house before her courage deserted her.

Her pumps had midheels—her last pair of high heels had been purchased for a senior class school dance—and her skirt and blouse were far from formal attire. But she felt inordinately dressed up. If Chance laughed, she thought with some panic while tripping across the compound, she would probably be crushed and lose every speck of courage, in which case, he would have another reason to laugh.

She suddenly stopped with gritted teeth. Dressing like this was ridiculous. She was a jeans and boots woman. Her curled hair was all right, her makeup was all right, too. But this outfit was going too far.

She ran back to her house and to her bedroom, where she got rid of the skirt, the blouse, the pumps, the slip and the nylon stockings. An impulse gripped her, exciting to contemplate. In the next instant, she took off her bra and panties, drew a bulky blue sweater over her head and put on her favorite denim skirt. She looked at herself in the mirror and saw the hopeful gleam in her eyes. If this meeting with Chance went anywhere, she was ready for it.

Thirteen

Chance was in the study when he heard someone coming through the back door of the house. He wasn't working or reading, but as he had little interest in Joe returning early from his weekly card game, he didn't get out of the big leather chair he'd been parked in—minus his brace—for a good hour.

He'd been wondering where his life was going, though he wasn't questioning its location; the ranch was home now. But the personal ramifications of living alone indefinitely were eating at him. He couldn't do without female companionship forever and he wasn't worried about finding a woman when the need got too great. But she wouldn't be Cleo, and that harsh fact was like a knife twisting in his gut every time it passed through his mind.

He'd been telling himself to grow up and come to grips with what was only obvious. Cleo wanted nothing to do with him. No woman could have made it any plainer. Maybe he would eventually find some comfort in knowing that Cleo didn't want *any* man, but right at the present he was suffering resentment and frustration, with an almost lethal amount of humiliation thrown in for good measure. The more he dredged up memories of chasing after Cleo like a horny kid, the deeper the humiliation went.

He was staring broodingly at his boots when he heard from the doorway, "Chance?"

His head turned slowly, and the face he showed Cleo contained none of the emotional upheaval of the past few days. "Yes?"

"May I talk to you for a few minutes?"

He gestured to a chair. "Sure. Sit down, if you want."

Crossing that room was a long walk for Cleo. She felt Chance's unblinking, unfriendly stare every inch of the way, and when she finally reached the chair, her descent to its padded cushion was awkward, and slightly embarrassing.

"What is it?" he questioned brusquely.

Cleo took a breath to begin. There was one very safe topic, and it was something that should be said in any case. "I'd like to thank you for what you did last night."

"You already did that, but you're welcome." Was that it? She'd come to thank him again? Deciding to forget Cleo hadn't made him immune to her. She looked especially beautiful today, wearing makeup and with her glorious gold hair curled. Her clothing was casual yet sexy. He liked her bulky sweater and certainly that denim skirt.

"I know you're angry with me, Chance."

He took a moment to contemplate the comment, and the inner bitterness he'd been living with rose to the surface. "I'm not sure angry's the right word. Try fool."

"Fool?" Cleo echoed uneasily.

"Me. I'm the fool, or I feel like one."

"Oh, but..." How strange that they would each condemn themselves for foolishness for being drawn to the other. Or for not being drawn. Or for behaving stupidly, for never doing or saying the right thing. At least Cleo saw herself in that vein. Chance shouldn't, though. "You're not a fool," she said. "I've never thought you were, and no one else on the ranch thinks so, either." She paused. "Rosie loves you."

"The feeling is mutual," Chance said crisply.

Cleo wondered if she weren't pale. Instigating a personal conversation with Chance when she'd been nothing but opposed to that very interaction had to be the most emotionally trying ordeal she'd ever attempted. Cutting herself off from the opposite sex for most of her adulthood had been a mistake in judgment, obviously, but never had that fact been more glaringly apparent than right now. A tangle of words, feelings and ideas were rushing through her head, but none seemed capable of reaching her lips.

On Chance's part, he was catching a glimpse of an astonishing idea: Was Cleo here to talk about them? Dare he even hope that was the case? He cleared his throat. "Where's Rosie now?"

"Visiting her little friend Darcy." Cleo's hands wound together and clenched in her lap.

"She was frightened by the fire last night. Is she all right today?"

Cleo managed a small nod. "Yes, she's fine. The dogs are fine." After a moment she added, "Everyone's fine... because of you."

Chance looked at her for several silent seconds. "You, too?"

Cleo knew this was her opening, his question being the perfect prelude to honesty, and she dare not let it pass. "No, I'm not fine. But not because of the fire. Because..." She bit her lip, trying hard to hold back emotion. He was outrageously handsome with his longer hair and weather-tanned skin, and she could hardly look him in the eye.

"Cleo, say what you're thinking," Chance pleaded. If she had any idea of what her coming in and attempting a frank discussion meant to him, she wouldn't hesitate for a heartbeat. Unless he was jumping to another false conclusion, he cautioned himself. He had so little confidence with Cleo. Again and again she had rejected his attentions, sidestepping his every effort to get them beyond their employer-employee status.

But instilled caution couldn't completely defeat that glimmer of hope Chance kept feeling. Cleo had something on her mind, and if it only concerned the ranch, would she be wearing makeup and perfume? Whatever subtle scent she had used was reaching his nostrils and fueling his imagination. His gaze remained on her while she underwent some private battle of her own, and he realized that whatever was going on behind her striking green eyes, this meeting wasn't easy for her.

"Chance, I'm so sorry," she finally said in a near whisper. "I've been living in the past, clinging to old hurts. I'm wondering now if I haven't been trying to hide from life out here. It was safe. New people rarely came along. Freezing out the few men I did meet was never a problem. I had Rosie, and Joe and Pete, and I truly believed no one else was needed."

She was twisting a button on her skirt while she spoke, and watching herself do it with the utmost intensity. Her eyes finally lifted. "None of the usual turndowns worked with you. I didn't know how to deal with that, or with you."

Chance knew he was staring, but he couldn't stop himself. Cleo's complex apology was mind-boggling, since she'd never talked about herself without tenacious prodding, wheedling and downright nagging on his part.

"We're very different people, Chance."

"Why do you think so?"

Cleo let go of the button to wave her hand. "You're educated. You've been . . . everywhere. You've seen and experienced things I've only read about, and probably a lot I haven't even heard about."

This was astounding for Chance. She *was* here to talk about them, and he had to forcibly squelch a sudden intense need to ease her discomfort through physical contact. He wanted to go to her, to lift her from the chair, to let her know by touch how moved he was by her apology.

Instead, he said, "Please don't say you feel inferior to me, Cleo. There's no reason for you to feel inferior to anyone, not about anything, but certainly not because I was fortunate enough to have someone else pay for my education, or to pick up the credit card bills for my traipsing around the world. I told you that before, Cleo. I told you who paid for everything." Chance leaned forward. "I look up to you, Cleo. I respected your knowledge and understanding of this country and the cattle business from the minute we met. If anyone should have felt inferior, it was me. What did I know about ranching when I got here? What do I know now that you haven't taught me?"

With a wistful smile, Cleo shook her head. "What you know can't be learned from someone else in a few months, Chance. You've got a feel for business I'll never have. You have vision and the courage to go after the big goal. You're going to make something out of this place that I never could have accomplished. I'd be willing to bet anything that the Kidd River Ranch will be very successful in a very few years."

Chance gave a short laugh. "Well, it might take a little longer than that, but thanks for the vote of confidence." His smile faded as his thoughts turned from the ranch to her. "Cleo, are you telling me you'd like to stay here?"

She was telling him a lot more than that, but she merely nodded and said, "I'd like to stay."

A deep-seated thrill increased Chance's pulse rate. She wanted to stay, which was what he wanted, as well. But stay as what? Employee? Friend? Lover? "You've been packing, haven't you?"

"Yes." She smiled. "The house is a mess. You can barely walk through it."

"You can stay as far as I'm concerned," Chance said quietly. "I never wanted you to leave in the first place."

"You told me to go."

"What I said was, go if you want to go. Cleo, no one can force another person to keep a job or live in one certain

place against their will. I tried to do that with you, didn't
I?''

"Um . . . you tried . . . something, but I'm not sure it was
to keep me on the payroll."

"Maybe we shouldn't be mixing apples and oranges,"
Chance suggested. "I wanted you on the ranch, but it was
mostly for my benefit. Not at first. At first I told myself
only an idiot would muck up a crucial working relationship
by chasing after his most valuable employee. But self-
directed lectures didn't hold up, Cleo. I just couldn't keep
my hands off you."

"And I couldn't say no. Not all the time." Cleo sighed.

Chance raised an eyebrow. "Do you think that's
changed?"

"My saying no?"

"No. My not being able to keep my hands off you."

She moistened her suddenly dry lips with the tip of her
tongue. "I can't answer for you. You . . . might have changed
toward me."

He sat back with an elation he had a hard time conceal-
ing. There'd been feelings between them all along, affection, desire, excitement, respect. But Cleo was just now
realizing that fact, or facing it, and he wondered what had
caused her incredible change of heart.

"Do you have any idea how really beautiful you are?" he
questioned softly.

A tremor rippled through Cleo's body, and she dropped
her eyes to her hands. "I'm not. Please don't exaggerate."

He shook his head, incredulous that she would have so
little confidence in her own appeal. "Why would I say that
if I didn't mean it, Cleo?"

"I . . . really don't know." Her gaze rose. "I'm not very
experienced with men."

None but Jake, Rosie's father, Chance thought. He didn't
want to feel jealousy because of Jake, but he did, realizing
at the same moment that if Cleo had loved more than one
man, Jake wouldn't be so important. It wasn't that he
thought Cleo still cared for the man; that had been a pass-

ing notion and no longer seemed credible. But she had loved Jake, and those weeks or months or however long their relationship lasted had left seemingly permanent scars, affecting her to this very day.

Anything she'd felt for Jake had been a sad waste of emotion. Chance could almost see the beautiful, eager girl Cleo must have been at the time. Brimming with wide-eyed trust and belief. Jake was the worst kind of person, committed and married, and living a single life behind his spouse's back. Cleo probably wasn't his only victim, if the truth be known.

But she was the one Chance knew and cared about. Cared *for*. Loved. Wanted in his life, at his side, sharing whatever the future held for either of them.

He maneuvered himself to his feet, walked over to her and held out his hand. Cleo stared at it. She dampened her lips. Tentatively her own hand rose from her lap. Almost gingerly she laid it upon his. His fingers flexed around it. Her thoughts stumbled over themselves, running wild. Her eyes lifted to meet his.

Declarations, promises and truths filled Chance's mind, but they were all *his* truths. Cleo was different today than she'd ever been, but what were her truths? He sensed an exciting but unfamiliar warmth from her, a new and delectable softness, and he wanted to trust his own instincts on her dramatic transformation. But one small pocket of doubt remained within him and demanded at least a moment of prudence. He had to *know* how she felt, had to believe it in his soul, and then he could speak of the future.

He tugged on her hand, gently, leaving her the option of refusing. The idea passed through Cleo's mind. She could say no again and still keep her job, still live on the ranch. Rosie would be happy about staying. Cleo, herself, recognized an enormous relief that she could empty the boxes strewn throughout the little house and then get rid of them.

This discussion with Chance had advanced far beyond any they'd previously had, but she felt no certainty about its conclusion. Only a certainty about Chance's desire, and a gladness within herself that he hadn't suddenly stopped wanting her.

She wanted him, too. Some dormant part of herself had awakened during the summer, Chance's doing. He'd been right when he suggested that he'd breached the wall she had erected around her emotions. He'd been accurate, also, about her guarding that self-protection and fighting anyone who tried to get past it.

Looking into Chance's blue eyes, Cleo thought about love. But he hadn't gotten near the subject and she didn't have the courage to introduce it, to be quite that bold.

But, indisputably, they had something special, and she needed it as she needed air and water.

Looking up at him, she got up from the chair. Chance's eyes darkened as he slowly drew her toward him. When their bodies met, when she laid her cheek on his chest and his arms closed around her, she released a drawn-out, emotional sigh. A sigh of acceptance, of acquiescence, of accord and harmony.

Chance heard it. He closed his eyes to savor this stunning moment of togetherness. Never had he felt so in tune with anyone. It was as if he had suddenly become a part of Cleo, an extension of her. The concept was startling. He honestly hadn't known a man could feel so connected to a woman.

He thought about asking if it was the same for her, but her arms had wrapped around his waist and she was snuggling closer. His own arms tightened. His pulse quickened. He wanted things out in the open with Cleo, but he suspected complete candor might take a little more time.

In the meantime they had this, a physical communion beyond comparison. His blood raced with the pounding beat of his heart, and he knew from the sensual movements of Cleo's body against his that she was feeling the same primitive call.

He sought her lips, tilting her chin up with a forefinger. Her mouth was giving, generous, and the kiss deepened until he felt a trembling in his arms and legs. He wanted to sweep her off her feet in a romantic gesture, to carry her up the stairs to his bed, but his back wouldn't permit any such grand flourish.

His hands rose to cup her face, while he studied the pinpoints of light and darkness in her eyes. "I never really thanked you for staying after my accident, did I?" he whispered.

"I . . . think you did," Cleo whispered back. "It doesn't matter." Her gaze roamed his features. "You have the most incredible mouth."

That "incredible" mouth touched hers again, caressing it in slow, drugging kisses that had her mind spinning. They had never kissed so slowly before. In almost every incident of intimacy between them, there'd been hunger and a speeding urgency.

The hunger was there, in his kisses, in hers, as was the urgency, but there was no haste, no hurry, and the more delicious pace had Cleo reeling. He was overwhelming; he'd been overwhelming since the day they met. She knew his body, its strength, its potency and the pleasure Chance could give her. Her physical need of him was all mixed up with love, with feelings that touched on his character, his personality, and encompassed respect, admiration and a sense of awe. Mingled with desire were memories, his friendship with Rosie, his unhesitating courage at entering a burning building to rescue two scruffy dogs because they meant so much to a little girl.

Cleo's own thoughts made her bolder, and she kissed Chance with utter abandonment while she unbuttoned his shirt. She pressed her mouth to his bare chest and felt his responsive shudder. His hands were suddenly under her skirt, but she only laughed softly at his startled exclamation when he encountered nothing but bare skin.

He knew, or strongly suspected, that Cleo wasn't in the habit of going without underwear, so her near nudity today had to be for him. His desire skyrocketed; it was the very first time she had done anything at all to lead him on, and it was incredibly exciting.

Cleo was dizzy and breathless and limp. The callused hand under her skirt shouldn't feel like velvet, but it did, and it knew so well how to incite pleasure. But her legs were becoming weak and unreliable, and if Chance and she didn't consciously leave this room, they would be making love on the floor. She nipped at his lips, whispering, "Maybe we should go upstairs."

Chance hastened to comply. With his eyes glittering hotly, he took her hand and led her from the study and to the stairs. It took only a minute to reach his bedroom. Inside, he closed the door and turned to take her in his arms.

His heart lurched, because she was already lifting her sweater over her head. Eagerly he started getting rid of his own clothes, but his eyes never left Cleo. He loved the firm, lean contours of her body, her small breasts and proud, rose-colored nipples. How could she think she wasn't beautiful?

Nude, they went to each other. His hands moved over her body, downward, then up again, stroking, making her skin tingle and her nipples pucker. He wove his fingers in her hair and drew her head back, and his mouth nestled into the exposed curve of her throat. She touched his shoulders, his arms, the back of his neck, and let her eyelashes droop and block out sight.

"Come," he whispered, and brought her to the bed, where he threw back blankets. He'd spent so much time in this bed that till this moment he'd been convinced he loathed it. Now it looked perfect, wide and long and designed for lovers.

Any latent inhibitions that Cleo had brought with her had vanished, though most were already vanquished before she entered Chance's house. Now she felt both weightless and heavy, a heady sensation caused by her newfound freedom from the past and the intoxicating rhythms of lovemaking.

Lying down, with legs and arms intertwined, they exchanged breathless kisses. Cleo's mind cleared for a moment. "Your back," she cautioned.

"I don't even know I have a back right now," he growled deep in his throat. He began kissing a trail to her breasts. "You're a fever in my blood, Cleo."

Her eyes closed on a husky sigh. "You're a fever in mine, Chance."

He groaned while sucking on her nipple, and then lifted his gaze to her face to whisper raggedly, "I feel like it's been ten years since our last time. I don't want to rush you, but I need you so bad, honey."

She was feeling the same desperation. "Rush me all you want."

He moved quickly because he had to. There were a hundred, a thousand, prickles of torment in his body, every one of them demanding release. He took the briefest moment for protection, then joining together was like heaven on earth for him. He burrowed his hands under her hips and kissed her lips, and began the joyous ride.

Her low moans were more arousing than the most erotic music. A truly passionate woman was a treasure, and in the dim recesses of his own passion-drugged mind, Chance thought of all the days and nights to come with Cleo in his bed. She must love him, she had to. She wouldn't be here, writhing beneath him, surpassing his own ardor, if she didn't.

He listened to her muffled sounds to see if she mentioned love, but his heartbeat was so strong and his breathing so ragged, he only grasped the intensity of her pleasure.

It was driving him to the edge, as was the explosive need in his own body. He couldn't control it any longer, and he went over praying Cleo was with him.

She was. Her powerful climax nearly blinded her, and she melted from the inside out, weeping quietly and clinging to Chance.

During the afterglow, Chance thought about the next step. They were united now, though he knew Cleo wasn't going to be the first to say so. That was all right; he didn't mind being the one to bring this to its best conclusion.

Smiling, he raised his head. "Now I know I have a back."

Cleo's eyes became concerned. "Are you in pain?"

"A little." Carefully he moved to the bed and lay on his back. But he turned his head on the pillow to see her. "It will never stop me from making love to you, Cleo. Only you can do that."

She pushed herself up to an elbow. "But you know I'll never stop you again, don't you?"

He brushed silken, gold hair back from her cheek. "I know it. When did you know it?"

"It's been brewing for quite a while, but this weekend brought it to a head." She looked into his warm and satisfied eyes. "The way I kept pushing you away seems a little silly now, doesn't it?"

"You had your reasons."

"Yes, I had my reasons."

He pulled her head down for a kiss, and her mouth moved temptingly on his. His eyes were smoky again when they broke apart. "Damn, you're sexy," he whispered.

She laughed shakily. "So are you. I guess that's what makes you so irresistible."

His expression sobered. "Am I irresistible to you, Cleo? Is that the reason you're in my bed right now?"

Her eyes darted from his. "It's . . . quite a substantial reason, don't you think?"

His reply came slowly. "Substantial . . . yes." He smiled suddenly. "Guess what we're going to do now."

Cleo laughed, huskily this time. "I don't think I need very many guesses, Chance."

He laughed with her. "We're going to make love again, sweetheart, but there's something else that needs doing first."

"Oh?"

"I'm going to help you get settled."

"As in unpacking all those boxes?" she questioned archly, not believing for a second that he was offering to tackle the many boxes cluttering her house.

"Well, yes, I guess you could put it like that. Come on."

Cleo watched him get off the bed with some amazement, then slid to the edge of it herself. "Well, all right, if you insist," she murmured, though she still had trouble believing he intended to do any unpacking.

They began dressing, stopping often for kisses. Cleo couldn't deny a unique happiness over the day, and yet a strange melancholy gripped her during the walk from one house to the other. They hadn't resolved anything, other than her staying on the ranch. Chance still wanted her, she still wanted him and she could feel herself getting closer to a long-term affair.

What alarmed her was the resignation she was also feeling. Staying at the ranch and keeping her job was final in her mind, but she had also made another decision without really meaning to. She'd remain at Chance's beck and call because she loved him. She had committed herself today as surely as though he had put a wedding ring on her hand, but there was no ring, of course. Nor any indication there ever would be.

That was probably her own fault. Her constant denials had obviously left an indelible mark on Chance, and maybe he simply couldn't bring himself to mention the word *marriage* again. Maybe someday, Cleo told herself with both sadness and hope.

They went into the small house and Chance took a look at the stacks of filled, partially filled and still empty boxes crowding the rooms. "I'd say you've been busy, honey."

Cleo followed him through the house with halfhearted enthusiasm. Her feelings for him went as deep as her own soul, and she knew now that his for her only lurked on the surface of true affection. The aftermath of lovemaking was leaving her feeling a little empty, and it didn't set quite right.

"I've got a great idea," Chance announced. "Why don't we have all of these boxes brought to the big house and unpacked there?"

"I can't do that!" Cleo gasped, genuinely shocked. "Rosie..."

"Loves me. You said so yourself." Chance put his hands on Cleo's shoulders.

"Listen to me, Chance," she said rather frantically. "I will not move in with you. Whatever relationship you and I have aside from ranch business has to be conducted with the utmost discretion."

"You're thinking we'll sneak around to see each other?" Chance questioned with a slightly raised eyebrow. "Like meeting after dark when everyone's sleeping? Or maybe taking the van for a drive?"

Cleo flushed. "Those are possibilities, yes."

"I'm not overly taken with the idea of hiding what we have, Cleo."

"But that's how it has to be! Rosie's so young, and I won't have her wondering about her mother's behavior."

"Nor will I," Chance said softly. "Cleo, don't you know I'm in love with you?"

She couldn't speak right away. There was a roaring in her ears, and she stared up at him with her mouth open.

"I love you," Chance repeated. "I'd like you to move into the big house as my wife."

"Ohmygod," she whispered.

"You're not really that surprised, are you?"

"I'm... floored. I thought you were coming over here to help me unpack."

"To get you settled, I think I said." He lifted his hand from her shoulder to her hair. "Cleo, it's so simple. Either you love me or you don't."

She was trembling, shaking like a leaf. "I...love you. Of course, I love you. But you never even hinted..."

"I hinted a dozen times," he rebutted gently. "Admit it. Didn't I talk about you and I growing old together?"

"Yes," she whispered.

"We're not going to do any more sneaking, Cleo. If you say yes, we're going to let the whole world know we love each other." He pulled her close, burying his face in her hair. "The smell of your hair turns me into a wild man, sweetheart. What's your answer? Should we set the date?"

"Yes," she said weakly.

"What did you say?"

"I said . . ." Tears sparkled in her eyes, but she was smiling all over her face when she tipped her head back and looked at him. ". . . *yes!*"

Chance, too, was grinning. "That's what I thought you said." Laughing, he squeezed her into a bear hug. "God, life is good."

They were both startled to hear someone knocking on the door. Their gazes met. "Who?" Chance asked.

Cleo's eyes widened. "Pete! I forgot about asking Joe to tell Pete to come by and talk to me today."

"Pete has the most uncanny knack of showing up at crucial moments in my life," Chance drawled.

"In mine, too," Cleo reminded with a chuckle. Slipping from Chance's embrace, she went to open the door. "Hi, Pete."

"Joe said . . ."

"Yes, I know. It was a false alarm, Pete. Everything's fine."

"You're not leaving, then?"

Chance came up behind Cleo to grin at Pete. "She changed her mind about leaving, Pete."

Pete's gaze went back and forth between the two of them, while a slow grin broke out on his face. "Glad to hear it, Chance, real glad. See you two later."

With the door closed, Chance put his arms around Cleo. "I wanted to tell Pete about us getting married, but figured you'd want to talk to Rosie before anyone else."

Cleo's eyes were shining like twin beacons. "She should hear it first." She spoke more gravely. "Chance, your doubts about Jake . . ."

"What I said only came out of jealousy, Cleo."

"You shouldn't be jealous of a bad memory. That's all Jake's been for many years, Chance."

"I know that now. Let's forget Jake, okay? Someday, should Rosie ask for information about her father, you might have to resurrect him. Until then, no one matters ex-

cept you, me and Rosie.'' Chance's mouth descended to Cleo's for a loving kiss that had them both breathless in seconds. Nevertheless, he was smiling slightly when he raised his head. "There *are* two other people who matter, Cleo, my brothers. We're going to have to arrange a meeting.''

"Whenever you say," Cleo whispered. With her hand on the back of his neck, she drew his head down to impishly murmur against his lips, "How would you like to try out *my* bed, handsome?''

He laughed deep in his throat. "I'm ready, willing and able, sweetheart.''

It was something she already knew. After all, they were pressed so tightly together, a straw couldn't have been wedged between them.

*   *   *   *   *   *

There are still two more SAXON BROTHERS *who have yet to meet their match. Look for Rush's Story,* MYSTERY LADY, *available in April—only from Silhouette Desire.*

Take 4 bestselling love stories FREE

Plus get a FREE surprise gift!

SILHOUETTE®

Desire®

JOAN JOHNSTON'S

HAWK'S WAY

SERIES CONTINUES!

Available in March, *The Cowboy Takes a Wife* (D #842) is the latest addition to Joan Johnston's sexy series about the lives and loves of the irresistible Whitelaw family. Set on a Wyoming ranch, this heart-wrenching story tells the tale of a single mother who desperately needs a husband—a very *big* husband—fast!

Don't miss *The Cowboy Takes a Wife* by Joan Johnston, only from Silhouette Desire.

SILHOUETTE *Desire*

COMING NEXT MONTH

#847 BEWITCHED—Jennifer Greene

Jock's Boys series

April's *Man of the Month*, Zach Connor, swore off family life long ago. But could he resist single mom Kirstin Grams and a matchmaking ghost who was intent on setting the two up?

#848 I'M GONNA GET YOU—Lass Small

Fabulous Brown Brothers

Tom Brown wanted Susan Lee McCrac, a honey-blond beauty with a streak of Texas stubbornness and a string of admirers. But he didn't want her just for now...he wanted her for always!

#849 MYSTERY LADY—Jackie Merritt

Saxon Brothers series

Sexy Rush Saxon was searching for riches, but found a floundering construction business and the last demure woman on earth. But Valentine LeClair held a secret she would never share with *this* ex-playboy.

#850 THE BRAINY BEAUTY—Suzanne Simms

Hazards, Inc. series

Egyptologist Samantha Wainwright had no time for an ex-Boy Scout doing a good deed. But for Jonathan Hazard, it wasn't just his job to protect this beauty...it was also his pleasure!

#851 RAFFERTY'S ANGEL—Caroline Cross

Years ago ex-agent Chase Rafferty had killed an innocent man. Now why was beautiful Maggie McKenna, the victim's wife, helping Chase get on with *his* life?

#852 STEALING SAVANNAH—Donna Carlisle

C.J. Cassidy needed to prove that he, was no longer a thief. But how could he when all he could think about was stealing Savannah Monterey's heart?

Silhouette

SPECIAL EDITION

That SPECIAL Woman!

MYSTERY WIFE
Annette Broadrick

She awoke in a French hospital—and found
handsome Raoul DuBois, claiming she was his wife,
Sherye, mother of their two children. But she didn't
recognize him or remember her identity. Whoever she
was, Sherye grew more attached to the children every
day—and the growing passion between her and
Raoul was like nothing they'd ever known before....

She's friend, wife, mother—she's you! And beside
each Special Woman stands a wonderfully *special*
man. It's a celebration of our heroines—and the men
who become part of their lives.

Don't miss **THAT SPECIAL WOMAN!** each month—
from some of your special authors! Only from
Silhouette Special Edition!

TSW494

As seen on TV!
Free Gift Offer

With a Free Gift proof-of-purchase from any Silhouette® book,
you can receive a beautiful cubic zirconia pendant.

This gorgeous marquise-shaped stone is a genuine cubic
zirconia—accented by an 18" gold tone necklace.

(Approximate retail value $19.95)

Send for yours today...
compliments of ▼ *Silhouette*®
™

To receive your free gift, a cubic zirconia pendant, send us one original proof-of-
purchase, photocopies not accepted, from the back of any Silhouette Romance™,
Silhouette Desire®, Silhouette Special Edition®, Silhouette Intimate Moments® or
Silhouette Shadows™ title for January, February or March 1994 at your favorite retail
outlet, together with the Free Gift Certificate, plus a check or money order for $2.50
(do not send cash) to cover postage and handling, payable to Silhouette Free Gift Offer.
We will send you the specified gift. Allow 6 to 8 weeks for delivery. Offer good until
March 31st, 1994 or while quantities last. Offer valid in the U.S. and Canada only.

Free Gift Certificate

Name: _____

Address: _____

City: _____ State/Province: _____ Zip/Postal Code: _____

Mail this certificate, one proof-of-purchase and a check or money order for postage
and handling to: SILHOUETTE FREE GIFT OFFER 1994. In the U.S.: 3010 Walden
Avenue, P.O. Box 9057, Buffalo NY 14269-9057. In Canada: P.O. Box 622, Fort Erie,
Ontario L2Z 5X3

FREE GIFT OFFER
ONE PROOF-OF-PURCHASE

079-KBZ

To collect your fabulous FREE GIFT, a cubic zirconia pendant, you must include this
original proof-of-purchase for each gift with the properly completed Free Gift Certificate.

079-KBZ